sT. BLAIR

CHILDREN OF THE NIGHT

E. W. SKINNER

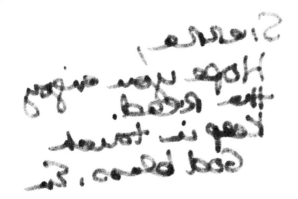

For Blair, a Godly daughter who inspires me by her love, talent and sense of humor.

I am blessed by you and I love you.

LIQUID AGONY

Sybille felt the burning ache of the concrete plank under her bare heels as she struggled to keep her balance. A tear streamed down her pale cheek and plunged off the apple curve to the abandon of a ten story free-fall.

Could she muster the courage to do the same? Couldn't she just as easily let go as hang on?

She felt anchored by invisible lead weights, as if there were thick chains tied around her heart that pulled at her lungs. It was hard to breathe. She closed her soft green eyes, feeling her brows tighten together. Her head pounding in a stabbing throb.

So many questions still unanswered... *What is it like to have someone really love you? Return your love? Look at you with longing? Desire you?*

A hiccupping sob brought forth a moan that bellowed from her mouth, causing her lower lip to puff in short bursts. She pressed the fingers of her right hand into the rib bones over her heart, wanting to rip it out. Feel herself deflate like a rubber ball. A watercolor kaleidoscope of fresh tears washed her vision.

Past relationships were not serious or sexual other than kissing and consensual caresses. It didn't seem to matter until... until she saw *him*. And now it was the one year anniversary of flirting across the subway car, watching him, listening to his soft baritone laugh… brushing against his thighs and hoping for him to catch her as the car stopped suddenly.

She couldn't understand what it was that drew her to him. Even though all they'd exchanged was a handful of words and a million unrequited glances, Sybille could only focus on what couldn't be.

How could she go on? Why couldn't she be with Mark? She barely knew him, but her heart needed to know him. Prescribed touch therapy didn't work. She wanted *his* touch.

The numbness in her ankles and calves felt as though she'd been standing for an eternity, though it had been less than an hour. She watched as another tear disappeared to join the foggy evening mist. She was raining down into a dampness that would be breathed in by warm lungs.

Could those below absorb her pain? Could this release of liquid agony cleanse the toxins of love lost? *But doesn't love have to be* experienced *to be lost?* Could she, at 17, really feel sorrow for a love she would never know? Or was there something else wrong with her? An emptiness that needed filling and Mark seemed to be the cure, but was he?

Or was it the routine, the restriction of choice that ate at her?

The dusk sky seemed to mirror the world's gray tones. The city's buildings appeared in mourning through the murkiness, their soldierly guard of residents an unnecessary obligation. They were the home front, the places of welcome and rest, stoic watchmen of the overcrowded metropolis. She saw the flash of a zeppelin in the distance.

The silver bubbles carried the government's Monument Patrol in their basket undercarriage over the city of Manhattan. Theirs was a bird's eye view of land and aquatic traffic. With the exception of aerial trolleys that provided maintenance crews access to their perches atop aging skyscrapers, transportation was limited to communal vehicles, bikes and foot traffic.

She envied the members of the Harbor Council who made daily trips around the island to protect the ferries and monuments. She looked down at the faint outline of ant-sized people bustling down the middle of 7th Avenue as bicyclists and rickshaw deliveries raced alongside pedestrians in a parallel lane.

"Need help," she whispered to anyone who might hear or respond. Fresh tears discharged in rapid succession.

Sybille moved to the right of the sill and turned sideways. She placed one foot in front of the other as a gust of wet fog draped over her slight five-foot seven body, pushing her soggy, shoulder length brunette locks against her thin face.

Her gray jumper was moist, clinging to her legs. She gripped the inside sill with her left hand twisted backward and touched her right toe to the frame of the left sill. She balanced on her left foot. This stretch felt good. She laughed nervously, thinking Crystal would wonder why she was doing ballet moves on an open window ledge. Her left ankle gave some as she tried to steady herself.

That was close. She clawed at the interior wood frame and a new ache formed under the nail of her left index finger.

Did she actually want to live? She was so confused.

The splinter dug itself deeper under her fingernail as she held tight with her left hand. *Damn, that really hurt!* She grabbed the top of the open window with her right hand and pulled the left hand to her mouth. She quickly clamped her teeth over the splintered wood and pulled it out of the sore flesh. As she did a red dot splashed on the interior window shelf.

She hadn't seen blood released before. It was quite beautiful, pooling in a dark kidney shape on the crackled finish.

Grabbing the open window with both hands she faced inside, but did not immediately recognize the sad, slender girl staring back from the glass. Sybille wanted to talk to her reflection, ask if the other girl felt trapped. Could she join her likeness? Could they escape together? Or would their new world become a pane of pain?

Evening security would soon find her. If she didn't jump, she might wish she had.

Her mother taught her from a small child to be good as the government was. Watchful eyes were always aware of her.

What if she just let go and fell backwards? Wouldn't it be better than seeing the ground rush up to meet her?

Her resolve faded and she hopped down to the tile floor inside, bending her head close to the blood droplet that leeched onto the aged structure. With her wounded finger, she smeared the crimson liquid in a heart pattern as another generous drop released itself. She continued to spread blood on the weathered ivory surface as chips of paint pulled off.

Did it matter if she played in the mess? Did *anything* matter?

The chips turned pink as she clawed at them, imbedding shards under her nails. The plaster below the wooden sill was weak. She pressed on the window sill again and it had some give. She wiggled it, wondering how she had not broken it when she'd found her way onto the ledge.

She grasped the sill with both hands under its lip and pulled up with a hard thrust. A startling POP followed and she stumbled slightly.

She peered inside the wall structure. The window frame revealed more wood, faded peach insulation and something blue. Imbedded between the beams and fiberglass she saw what appeared to be pressed paper wrapped in a blue skin.

She retrieved the keycard from her right jumper pocket, the green digital light flashed 9.14.2202 Night Meal. She clicked it off and began digging with it to release the concealed item. What could it be? Why would such a thing be hidden inside a window ledge?

The blood was sticky and coagulating under her nails and she didn't want to ruin her treasure, so she alternated sucking on the painful finger and wiping her hand on her jumper, which was striped in dark swipes of blood and chalky paint residue.

The grind of chains and metal below brought her back to reality. Someone had begun their ascent to the 10th floor. She would be in trouble for sure. She moved quickly, slicing, sawing and tugging.

Her heart quickened, feeling the chug of the elevator gnashing its way up the ancient structure. Blood-soaked paint flecks and stark white plaster chips dotted the floor and baseboard around the window.

This city had survived more than 400 years of change and this building alone more than 200 years. History was built on ownership and, while public housing was once associated with a lower quality of life, the reverse was now reality. No longer was it acceptable to tear down and construct new living spaces for aesthetics or a class of people. Terms of use and historic value were applied and by utilizing aged housing, if functional, the restoration of interior and exterior spaces was priority one.

Sybille heard the lurch of the elevator and groaning of the metal gate folding open just twenty feet or more behind her. With the thumb and middle finger of her right hand she grasped the thin booklet and gave a hard yank. It pulled free.

At that moment it was as though an invisible force swirled around her in a tornado of energy and the whole place quaked in an instant as though a rocket were set off. Her ears popped, her vision became laser sharp as she stumbled to catch herself and— almost as quickly as the energy hit her   it left.

She blinked, heard a voice and saw gold specks in her right eye's peripheral vision. She closed her left eye to focus her right eye and she could see someone! It was a female figure, fuzzy and gold.

"I'm here with you," Sybille heard audibly in her right ear.

She also heard the steps approaching from behind.

She turned quickly to see who or what she would encounter. It was better to face her nemesis as she felt blindly for the keycard along the rough surface of the ledge behind her. Was it there? The flickering in her right eye was diminishing and her heart skipped a beat as her now tender fingers touched the thin card, dislodging it from the sill.

Too late…

She turned in time to see the keycard fly out the open window, a dancing feather just out of reach.

RUSHING UPON HER

Sybille splayed her fingers and reached out both palms in hopes of making contact with the card when she heard, "Sybille!"

It seemed the stern voice carried enough of a gust to push the card higher and further.

How was she going to get back in her apartment? Would it matter?

She dropped the book into her pocket and turned to face her neighbor, Beatrice, who was marching toward her.

Relief. It wasn't security. She might have a chance to read the contents after all. She needed to wash off the window casing and put the sill back in place before DNA was secured, but where could she go? Or would Bea report her?

"Syb?" The athletic, yet elderly blonde woman approached. "My, my. What happened?"

Sybille just stared at the woman and said nothing.

"Did someone hurt you?"

"My keycard fell out the window." She wondered if Bea felt the quake, but she didn't want to ask.

"Oh, that's going to be a challenge. You're Baker and Abner Malone's child, correct?" The older woman seemed more perturbed by the thought of getting a replacement than the mess of blood and damage to the window sill. "Well there was no reason for you to destroy the building in your frustration! But why was the window open?"

Beatrice's eyes narrowed as she stared at the younger woman, then back at the situation before them.

Sybille nodded in agreement, she was a Malone but refused to address the situation. "Could I freshen up in your apartment? I need to ... before I go to the council for a new key."

"Well, I'll loan you a jumper, but you MUST return it, you can't go looking like that. I AM NOT happy you've made me an accessory."

Suddenly the realization of standing on the ledge hit Sybille. How had she done it? She felt as though her knees would buckle at that moment.

What had she gotten herself into? Why was Beatrice mentioning her parents? The gold flecks were twitching in her right eye again and she felt both eyes getting heavy; she could hear the older woman but didn't follow what she was saying. She felt weak.

Bea was so preoccupied with the scene that she didn't notice the younger woman swaying. "….but I'm not going to report you. It would serve neither of us to spend the evening filing behavior complaints. I'll call maintenance after you clean the hallway."

Bea grabbed Sybille's wrist and turned her hand over. "You're going to soak, I hope." Then the older woman went quiet; the cold dampness of Sybille's skin was alarming. The girl was either ill or faint.

Sybille's mind snapped back to reality. This kept her from dropping.

It was all rushing upon her now. The desperation and the contemplation of ending her life, the inner loneliness and the longing.

She took a deep breath and began to sob softly. "What will you..?"

"Don't. There will be no weeping," Beatrice demanded.

Sybille nodded in agreement.

"Take some tonic and compose yourself. Why is your eye twitching?"

Tonic? She hadn't had tonic since her preteens. Sybille knew it to be calming oil, as her mother put it, empowering citizens with a *sense* of choice, and while there was no harm keeping it in one's residence or sharing it, it was the last of the government's approved self-regulating medications. All controlled substances had been outlawed more than 100 years earlier.

Sybille rubbed her right lid. "Happens when I'm nervous," she lied. It was so foreign for her to make up an untruth. She wondered how she managed to speak it.

Then she noticed Beatrice looking at the outline of her pocket. Sybille turned away sniffling. *Take tonic! Beatrice was calling her weak … and… why not? The evidence was right in front of them. Not only had Sybille destroyed property, but she had an illegal item… and she had no idea what was going on with her eye.*

Beatrice indicated Sybille's blood smeared garment with a stern once-over. "You're not putting that jumper in my laundry order!"

"I won't, I'll get you one of mine… can I change, please?"

FLOW OF PRESSURE

"You're snoring," Beatrice poked Sybille's shoulder as she walked past the younger woman. Sybille had no more than sat on the chaise when she dozed off.

Beatrice's apartment was like Sybille's and every other residence in the building. Government issued light blue sofa, a cream colored lounger, a blue molded plastic rocking chair and a beige oval coffee table, accented by beige walls and a small fireplace for winter nights when the old building's furnace wasn't working well. Approved personal photos, timed for each shift of residents, projected on the wall above the couch one after another—a slideshow offering individuals the visual sense of a unique existence.

Each bedroom contained one single bed with a trundle for partnering that could be pulled up to form a double bed. The bedspread was stock issue navy blue cotton with beige polka dots; there was one head pillow and one body pillow per resident. In the room's corner was a garment rack for hanging clothing and six rounded cubes for folded undergarments, athletic wear and shoes.

Sybille lifted her chin off her collar and stretched her arms upward. She tried to sit up straight in the lounger but her lower back was tight from standing on the window ledge. She was exhausted, and would definitely set off meters if she didn't eat and get real rest soon.

Beatrice Croce lived with her husband's brother, Frank Croce. Her husband Salvatore had died more than eleven years earlier and they both found solace sharing a place.

Frank was at the theatre for a few hours and Beatrice was concerned he'd be shocked by Sybille's appearance and call security.

"Please take this," Beatrice handed the younger woman an identical jumper and a pair of shoes. "I don't know how you'll feel in my shoes? ... And fix your hair, Frank will be back shortly and we have to convince him to allow you to sleep here."

Sybille had already been down the hall a few times to see if her roommate Crystal Lundgren had arrived home, to no avail. So her only solution was to stay with Bea for the evening. Sybille nodded and rubbed her puffy eyelids with the fist of her left hand. Then she noticed the caked blood under her fingernails. "Mind if I shower?"

"Please do."

Sybille padded to the small but functional bathroom with the folded garment held to her chest.

"May I read it?" Beatrice called out to Sybille.

She closed the door and pretended not to hear what Bea was saying.

Once undressed, she stood before the mirror staring at her flat stomach, lean ribcage and nearly flat, solid breasts. Women's bodies didn't appear all that different, unless they were pregnant. She tried to imagine her stomach stretched by a baby, and wondered if she would ever find a suitable partner…

Then it hit her, *Mark*. He was the whole reason she was in this situation.

She turned away, embarrassed at her naked self as if he were watching too. She stepped into the shower and turned the cold water dial and then the hot, waiting for the temperature to even out as the pipes whistled to the flow of pressure. The rising steam refreshed her. She washed hurriedly, not wanting to disappoint Beatrice, the only person who could protect her right now.

She turned the temperature up and enjoyed the sting of the water's pleasureful pain scalding her scalp, neck and shoulders, rinsing the stains of misery from her hands… but not her heart.

Then she felt it again, a piercing in the middle of her chest, shooting straight through her breasts and stopping deep in her abdomen. Her knees wobbled as the throbbing seemed to intensify and she shut off the hot water first, letting the cold take her breath before turning it off. She leaned against the tile, hugging her thin frame and feeling the closeness of his hip next to her in the subway car. The pain returned.

She had to stop thinking of him!

Toweling off, she put on the undergarments and outer day garment, knowing she would have to sleep in it for the next several hours. There would be no opportunity to get into her own apartment that night.

She wrapped her hair in Bea's blue terry towel and pulled the book from the pocket of her bloodstained jumper. Her fingernails, though chewed up, were now clean and bright pink flesh shone under the nails.

Sybille slipped into Bea's shoes. They were snug. The foam lining had enough give to keep them from causing much pain, she hoped. She stood next to the door and opened the book to the first page.

Blair's diary and vision

Hi Sybille,
You found it! So glad…

Stunned, she snapped the book shut.
How?

A new feeling of surprise quickly erased her sadness. "I don't understand?!" Her eyes welled up and a smile quivered to her lips.

She held the diary to her heart. Her mind raced, she wanted to read and devour it all, but it was so thin it would be consumed quickly.

And what about Bea? She asked if she could read it…

She opened it again.

> Hi Sybille,
> You found it! So glad…

Warmth enveloped her. The twitching began again and she closed her left eye. With her right eye she strained to see what was making the brilliant flickering in her peripheral vision, but when she opened both eyes it was gone. She looked at the book and wondered who this message was from? Is Blair a boy? Or girl?

She slid down the door and soaked in the feeling she couldn't name. She couldn't even *comprehend* it.

Did she have an admirer? Could someone have planted this with the intent of a rendezvous?

Was she destined to go out on the window ledge?

It gave her purpose. Hope. She took a deep breath. *Would someone set her up?* Deductive reasoning taught her to avoid negative conclusions and live in a state of peace. This didn't compute. She opened the book again and read:

> Hi Sybille,
> You found it! So glad you did. Well, I hope your name is Sybille, because that's what God brought to me. So it's weird, I…

*Humph, Good was spelled wrong…*Sybille was startled by the pounding at the back of her head.

"Are you okay?" Beatrice knocked hard and Sybille was shaken. "I'm going to open the door if you don't respond."

She snapped the book shut and tried to clear her throat. "I'm changing…" she managed, then held her mouth to stifle the sob building inside. She dropped the book into her borrowed jumper's pocket and stood quickly, wiping away tears with the back of her hand. She pinched her cheeks and forced a practice smile. Her lip trembled.

Who are you Blair? Sybille wondered. Her right eye began to twitch again as she stared at herself in the mirror.

Could this be hope? Or was she just asking for trouble by having the diary?

She would have to decide quickly. Very quickly.

BACK TO THE WALL

Sybille, Bea and Frank enjoyed an evening meal at the cafeteria across from their apartment building.

Frank didn't seem to have a problem with the girl staying for one night. He was quite amused at the tale Sybille spun about the keycard flying out the window. She explained that she was gazing at zeppelin traffic in the evening sky and longing to ride in one when she opened the window to feel the night air and the card released from her grasp. Bea even laughed, as though she hadn't remembered the destruction of the window frame and the blood-stained jumper.

Frank reminded Sybille of her father. Both men had a warm, low-key sense of humor.

Though her parents Baker and Abner Malone resided in the city, the trio only shared occasional outings to the opera or city concerts. Sybille longed for her childhood years of "family living", playing dominoes, cards and sharing story time.

Frank amused her. He had a grand way of sharing his 60 year adventure as a Monument Guard.

"The administration should reopen the dirigible terminal for the entertainment value, though it would be impossible to meet the demands of such a large population," he chuckled. Frank's square olive-toned face framed a dimpled chin, straight hook nose and deep brown eyes. He missed riding in the zeppelin's gondola.

Bea, too, revealed her times flying with her husband Salvatore, Frank's younger brother and how they were all employed by the Monument Society. Their family was a part of the administration's security.

Bea added with a smile, "Once in the Society, always in the Society."

Sybille realized both were enforcement officials and could easily have filed charges against her. Why were they accepting a young person like herself? A possible cancer to civil obedience and an insurgent to the administration's prosperity? A twitchy-eyed girl who might pose a greater health threat? Plus Bea knew about the book, yet she didn't challenge her. Could Bea have planted the book? Was Bea actually Blair?

"So Blair," she said to Bea.

"Bea."

"Sorry Bea, what is your favorite monument?"

Bea took a long hard look at the girl. Frank observed them both as a loudspeaker announcement broke the stillness. "Thank you for dining, we'll now be serving the next rotation, please bring your salver to the exit. Tomorrow's menu rat stew and rolls."

"Yum!" Sybille said. "I never understood why they called the vegetable dish ratatouille and the stew rat stew?"

They all stood.

"To be continued," Frank winked at her and nodded at Bea. "We'll have to do this again," he said, "though I'm a vegetarian. You enjoy that stew tomorrow."

Sybille wasn't sure if they were just being nice; she wasn't about to challenge them after they had agreed to shelter her overnight. They all grabbed their trays and proceeded to the exit.

Sybille slept in Bea's and Frank's lounger and awoke to the sounds of the coming shift change.

Each morning at just shy of 6 a.m. the Dayshift residents of her building prepared to depart their apartments for the incoming Nightshift. All buildings and apartments had dual sets of residents. Sybille and Crystal cohabited with Reggie and Julia Rowe and their son, Timmy, while Bea and Frank shared their apartment with Joe and Anne Ellis.

Sybille still needed to get a key replacement during the course of the day and get rid of the soiled jumper. She also needed to grab her roommate Crystal before she left their apartment.

"Thanks Bea, I have to catch Crystal." She rushed out with the soiled jumper folded and tucked under her left armpit, not acknowledging their goodbye.

She looked down the hall and saw some Dayshift people getting on the elevator. "Please Crystal, don't be gone," she muttered.

She also had to find a place to hide the book. It would be picked up by body scanners at the industrial complex. She saw the door open a brief moment and then shut. She knocked, "Crystal, have you left yet?"

A black man opened the door and smiled at her, a little boy hugged his leg. "Crystal just passed you. We got home ten minutes early and she met me in the lobby, I hope you don't mind?"

"Reggie," she realized he thought she was being polite by knocking. The law provided that once a shift's residents had vacated, the next shift could occupy the living quarters early. Sybille was officially locked out till 6 pm when the Nightshift went to work. Sleep hours for each shift were compulsory, while play hours were to be spent building relationships, socializing and enjoying culture. *If she had her key she could have just opened the door* because she was still within her key's activation time. "I need to put aside my laundry order…"

"You know they'll pick up dirty and drop off clean tomorrow when they do the weekly inspection," Julia called out. Julia was Reggie's life partner and she slept in Sybille's room while their son,

Timmy slept in the solarium and Reggie had his choice of Crystal's room or bedding with Julia.

"Ok, thanks." Sybille mumbled. Reggie shut the door. *What was she thinking? Julia believes she wants to put her hamper out, if she carried in the blood stained garment that could draw attention. Where would she put it and the book?*

Sybille looked down the hall and rolled her eyes. "Back to the wall."

She moved quickly down the corridor, pushed up the sill, placed the book back in its slot and gently put the ledge back in place. *That didn't make sense either, it had been repaired already? And yet she could still push the sill up easily?* She didn't have time to ponder it any further, she had to figure out what to do with the jumper.

Bea's intercom buzzed and Sybille heard the older woman as she was half in and out the door. "We'll be right down," she told her cohabs.

Sybille rushed over, holding the garment out. "Can you…?"

Bea gasped. "I told you no!" But she knew there was no time.

Frank glanced at Bea, as if for the first time understanding there was more going on than either Bea or Sybille had admitted.

"Is this necessary?" he asked.

"Yes. Last favor. Promise." Sybille's eyes pleaded with them both.

Bea grabbed the item and encouraged Sybille and Frank to hurry down the hall while she dashed back into the apartment.

Bea was going to place the garment in her hamper when she saw the fading orange embers in the fireplace. She grabbed a poker to maneuver the folded garment into a position where it would hopefully be consumed before Joe and Anne could detect it. She placed a small cut of timber on top. It appeared as though she was being neighborly. She hastened to the door.

"We'll be late. Everyone, move along," she said.

YEAR 2201

Sybille and Crystal each held the center pole of the subway car as they rocked back and forth with the sway of the vehicle.

Both young women were dressed in customary Dayshift-issue pale gray wool/cotton jumpers and white three-button pullover blouses. The tops were sleeved 100% cotton and fit over the body with a button mid-chest, a button just above it, and one at the collar for cold weather. All blouses were long in the body, one-size-fits-all for government standards and enough give if one's weight were to increase slightly.

It was Sybille who helped the Fabric Council develop the new jumper material from retired garments. The innovative fabric worked in diverse climates and gave the New Year a crisp look.

The garments were made from recycled uniforms in government storage and processed to minimize damage to the environment and make the administration less dependent on the Agricultural Council's cotton reserves.

It had been more than ten years since the council gave approval for a fabric modification, much less a design variation. The wool added insulation while the cotton helped the fabric breathe and the triple-seam reinforced garments held up for a three year lifespan. So at sixteen, Sybille was thrilled to have her first new look since she was a child.

The grays were stock issue and it was her hope to add color to future fabric plans. Each shift had to be consistent, hers was light gray and the passengers who were going to work on the Nightshift wore darker grays. All citizens were fit with custom-molded shoes for durable wear and engineered support. The shoes matched the shift's attire with women wearing deep foam-lined pumps and men in dress vinyl slipons. Both shifts had gray running shoes, tops and shorts for required physical recreation. Heavy winter coats and sweaters were issued each September and returned to the Council in April for laundering, disinfecting and storage.

Crystal was in charge of the feasibility study to see if adding an additional garment to each shift would expand the three year life of the customary issue. Undergarments, work clothing, athletic apparel, two pair of shoes and a nightshirt were the sum total of each person's wardrobe. Crystal and Sybille really wanted a weekend garment for theatre and team sporting events, but were denied the opportunity to submit design sketches thus far.

The government provided two costume events yearly where all citizens had the opportunity to dress for a community banquet and register for the garment of their choice six months prior. Sybille and Crystal got first wardrobe pick for the Semi-Annual Good Gala Manhattan. They managed the team maintaining the Council's costume closet.

Sybille glanced at the cute Nightshift passenger joking with his friend. She hadn't seen him before and she wondered if Crystal had noticed him. Crystal was very impressionable and seemed to like everything Sybille did, to a point of frustration. Sybille was cautious not to say anything to her. If Sybille liked a boy, Crystal would like him, too.

Crystal turned and looked over her shoulder. "You staring at those guys?"

"No." Sybille laughed.

"You were," Crystal accused. "Sy, I know you and it's about time you find a life partner."

"You want to be my partner, Crystal?" Sybille joked.

"We both know you have no physical attraction to women. Otherwise…" She gave Sybille a wink.

"And I have no physical attraction to anyone on our shift."

"Yet," Crystal corrected. "And you better keep your voice down. We don't need to be held for questioning."

"You are too concerned, Crystal." Sybille didn't think anyone would take them seriously.

"You are too bold, Sybille. We're getting too descriptive outside of Salon."

Sybille rolled her eyes. "We're allowed to talk Crystal. We don't have to be at a soiree to have an opinion."

"Ok, let's not go there, Sy." Crystal kissed the air in treaty.

Sybille kissed the air, too and turned back to gaze at the guy with jet black hair, aqua blue eyes and a large white cubed-teeth smile. He was so handsome… and wearing the wrong color uniform. She stood mesmerized and tried to listen to his conversation.

She caught the name Mark, it was a beginning. Sybille felt a stirring as he turned and smiled at her, then back to his conversation.

"We're not at the zoo," Crystal poked Sybille.

"It's called animal magnetism."

Just then a small insect flew around Sybille's head and darted through the subway car.

Eston Cote addressed his orientation students. Eston was a lean, physically fit thirty with a handsomely chiseled face, soft black hair, emerald eyes and a medium build. Male or female, they seemed to stare at him without knowing it. Eston was but a fraction of his parent's beauty. Their heritage: Region 78 royalty.

"Goodness requires entertainment," Eston walked to the side of the podium. "The citizens of the current age have little historic knowledge of past societies other than what Goodness deems necessary. Our society's knowledge is focused on vocational education, work, entertainment, social interaction in communal settings and dependence on the World Goodness Alliance or Global Good. Gone are individual elected leaders and the public policy they vetoed, bullied or lobbied..."

A young woman raised her hand, "Are we supposed to know these terms or remember them? I'm not sure I understand elected..."

Eston smiled. "You shouldn't know these terms. In fact, this is confidential. As my protégés' in GG, I want you to have a rudimentary knowledge of how society evolved. This is the way I was taught."

He was relaxed in his approach and moved to the back of the room. He wanted them to focus forward. When he spoke of the government he was very distinct in pronouncing the initials of Global Good as Gee-Gee. He wanted his students to center their attention on the projected wall and not himself. He was a restless, yet patient leader who expected excellence in his team.

"Some knowledge will remain with you should you need it. But please," he walked over to the young woman, the only female in the group and gently placed her hand on the scanner, "keep your right hand on the scanpad and your keycard in place as I speak."

She moved her olive-toned hand on the pad and a green light lit.

"Thank you." He returned to his presentation and clicked a pocket remote. An image of happy people flashed on the wall. "Goodness keeps the masses entertained, happy, engaged, positive, and productive. Entertainment keeps our creative juices flowing. We admire our entertainers but we do not elevate them to a higher social status. We dine with them and cohabitate with them..."

A young man raised his hand. "Why point it out?"

Eston smiled, "Because, it wasn't always like that. There was a time when entertainers had special privileges. You don't want to repeat a mistake."

"How would any of us do that?" The young man asked.

"I thought similar at your age. Now, I'm in a position that I could recommend changes, not that GG would agree with them, but knowing what failed keeps me from making an error." He clicked another picture into view. "If you could hold your questions and keep your hands on the scanpads."

Eston looked for their acknowledgement before proceeding. He wanted to introduce them to their peers in the three other Quad headquarter regions via satellite, but not until day two. Each office was conducting similar training with a select group of eight young people around the world, thirty-two in all.

"Actors today have training, regular table reads, rehearsals for shows and performances. Auditions aren't necessary as all actors have a set number of shows. There is no down time. There are an equal number of actors/actresses and performances per shift to keep all citizens amused and enlightened. The same goes for directors, stagehands and all related jobs."

Eston had personally selected the eight young citizens before him out of five hundred, each when they were only five-year-olds. Eston had just been 18 and in similar training as they were today when he made *their* selection. He reviewed audits of the children and tracked their progress and achievements throughout their developmental years. Each had a secret he provided them, and based on their ability to keep the secret he was now grooming them for Quad support.

Eston stopped and looked at his audience. They were focused, waiting. He continued, "Materialism or personal wealth created an imbalance of power and it was greed that killed much of that prior civilization. The surviving masses of 2100 were impoverished."

The young woman interjected again, "How does one contract greed?"

"It's a desire to possess and attain things selfishly."

"Not sharing?"

"That's a simple way to put it. And the majority around the globe, who died of greed, left a population behind that had no knowledge of their gluttony."

Another student raised a hand. "People had different ways of living?"

"Exactly," Eston said. "The surviving people were desert nomads, street dwellers and homeless…"

Another young man's mouth flew open. "Homeless?"

Eston took control. "I realize this is all new to you and it was a different world. Please hold your questions."

He continued. "The survivors were sickly, dying and emaciated people who got a chance to start over. And so did the remnants of their governments. The leaders who endured were mostly commoners who fought for social responsibility and tried in vain to stop greed. They were left to rebuild the world economy with the poor, unskilled castoffs. The new regime made sure that everyone would be equal."

He went on to share that the markets would not be repeated as publicly traded instruments that would divide people. But instead the markets would be deemed as organic foods, raw materials, labor and commodities that could sustain a global environment.

Trades that built industrial nations were soon challenged by a lack of talent. So elders who were once relegated to nursing homes were tapped for their expertise and returned to the workforce to develop skilled labor, Eston acknowledged.

"Age was no longer a reason to stop honing or developing one's self," he looked to seeing if they understood.

"Retirement took on a whole new meaning in a new world. One may retire from their position to one of a lesser position in the same industry, but not to rest. Instead these experts assisted the generations coming in with significant information and education. These Sage specialists kept fit alongside their youthful peers. They weren't revered, but equal." He moved beside the female student. "Everyone has a job to do until they expire."

She looked up at him and nodded. Eston smiled at her and moved on.

He was proud that the students were inquisitive. It gave him hope and confirmed he had selected the best. He was actually glad they persisted in asking questions and understanding.

He continued, "The *Society of Goodness* replaced world religion. All churches, synagogues, mosques and temples were converted to Goodness Centers for citizens to gather and enjoy art and entertainment. Remaining factions that attempted to hold on to their faiths…"

He paused.

He saw no benefit in explaining that Goodness Peace Doctors exterminated the faithful so the rehabilitated survivors wouldn't have to fight religious zealots or be influenced by their rituals and traditions. He couldn't imagine this ever happening again, given the evolution of civilization and their ability to cope without attachments to deities. Hundreds of years of peace was proof enough.

"Moving on… While you've never seen them, arms, weapons and ammunition are buried. All missile silos have been abandoned. Code that."

He wanted them to have a code in their microchips if needed. He would encode later but the terms would be in their keycards should the future require this data.

"Only Peace Ministers and Global Good have encrypted codes in their memory banks. Peace Minister became an accepted term in the transition as the religious attempted to adapt to the Goodness doctrine, but generations later we have changed to the term Entertainment Minister, however the term Peace Doctor has endured with time." Eston moved to the front of the room.

The room had light gray carpeted walls and enough furniture for the purpose of Eston's teaching. A functional space. The information he provided and collected was secure in GG North Headquarters.

"Yes," he pointed to the young woman again.

"Religious," she said, "Will you be coding that? I'm not sure I would understand… If someday I am in your shoes."

He nodded and continued, "Peace Doctors were the first responder field physicians who rescued many of the afflicted of 2070. The world governments surmised that entertainment and community would end a citizen's isolation and reliance on self."

Eston motioned again for the young woman to place her hand on the scanner.

"I will," she said, "when you code the term religious."

The young men were all staring at her. They said nothing.

Eston was firm. "You're training here, all of you are training here … each one of you … is to assist the Quad. Not question, demand or instruct, but to listen, understand and be engaged."

She placed her hand on the scanpad. The green light lit.

Eston continued. "Global Good wanted people to increase their skills in neighboring, learn a trade and continue to incorporate the goodwill aspect of faith-based practices. These practices along with the new world order, Good, would give society a sense that they were and are cared for by a higher authority and eliminate the need for religious factions and religion. Code that."

She smiled at him.

He addressed a young man with a raised hand.

"Did they wear gray, too? Or did they dress like the costumes we wear at galas?"

Eston laughed. "Good question. Uniforms replaced fashion. Gala costumes and theatrical costumes are modeled after the fashions of prior civilizations."

The female student asked for a break. Eston excused them for ten minutes. They left their keycards on the palm scanners, stretched and used the facilities within the confines of the secured training room.

When they resumed Eston explained how government-issued apartments replaced homes. Public transportation replaced cars. Junk foods were replaced with dietary mandates. Kitchens and food preparation were left to the experts. Apartments only contained the essentials of bedroom/solarium, sitting/game room and bathing facilities. Dining was done at the local cafeteria or supper club. Any remaining obese individuals were quarantined until their weight met requisite standards for their height, age and sex. As the economy grew, the masses were rewarded with needed surgeries and enforced treatments to build a healthy populace—both mentally and physically. Cosmetic procedures were required for those born with birth defects to provide emotional support for the victim and society.

Beauty treatments and cosmetic procedures were compulsory to give the general public an even playing field. Obvious differences that could cause insecurities or distract others were corrected. Harelips, birthmarks, moles, lesions, skin tags, enlarged noses, thin lips, chin structuring and aesthetic dental procedures were all part of regular health maintenance.

Comfortable loose attire provided a modest illustration of the government protocol. Women were lean and men trim. Maintaining regulated weight also meant that breasts and hips were smaller with less volume due to decreased fatty tissue, and cancers were few. Only in pregnancy did a woman's appearance change with any significance, and her maternity uniform was bright green for

Dayshift and dark green for Nightshift. Respect for fetal citizens was a priority to a decimated society.

Healthcare became a precedence to restore the nations destroyed by natural and man-made disasters, as well as the Bacterial Plague of 2070. Unsafe, unregulated personal communication devices that slaughtered millions worldwide via brain cancers were outlawed. Suicide rates that once rose as families realized their reduced mortality and refused to live a life apart from loved ones were nonexistent.

The war in the economy that took savings and banking to depressionary lows, stripped incomes, left homes abandoned by the millions as citizens huddled in ghettos for scraps from charity food drops would never be repeated.

Sadness, depression, despair, isolation and autonomy were no longer tolerated. Happiness, health, safety, and harmonious cohabitation were the directive for all citizens and each person was micro-chipped—as their ancestors had predicted might happen.

It was impossible to run one world without the simple technology. Flat cardreaders or keycards replaced currency and provided each resident with data, reminders, meal procurements, entertainment access and entrance to one's residence as well as resource information. Along with the microchip in the palm of each person's right hand, the government was able to track their citizens' interests and activities.

Procreation was mandated to re-populate the planet.

It worked. Too well.

Access to improved healthcare produced population overcrowding and there were few suitable places for all to reside in the *Goodness* infrastructure. Two distinct shifts were created for the 24-hour society. A Thirdshift held the offenders, the imprisoned, the infirmed, the physically and mentally-challenged who were not surgically-redeemable or learning-able and/or any person who threatened society's quality of life. The two priority surface shifts needed workers to generate and maintain power resources to keep their society running.

Eston stopped. He wondered how the world had ever managed under the archaic practices of letting people make their own decisions and choose their own jobs. It had to be chaos for the prior government to know that their talent was just wasting away doing mundane tasks until death, because they had a *choice*.

Eston wanted to be careful with his terms. "Any wrong is managed and offenders tried and corrected by removal. Removal to the Thirdshift is equal to prison in prior civilizations. However, we don't use prison as a standard term as we feel GG has evolved in the treatment of offenders. Those "moved" by an unseeing populace are actually in a phase of "correction." In many cases, those closest to the offender are moved, too, to avoid questions and rebellion by their family."

A young man asked, "Do cohabs and coworkers assume the move as a position transfer?"

Eston nodded, "Often times, those around wouldn't be aware of offenses as the Peace Doctors would score threats on multiple modalities. An examination tally could result in an arrest, trial and removal or 'transfer' of a societal risk."

Given these young people were now part of the Quad, he would be placing them in work details that suited their talents and when necessary, he would enlist their feedback on the activities they observe. They needed to blend in and some of the training would be dormant in their memories as this new awareness could create an overwhelming sense of public responsibility. It would not be possible to release them to work detail if the information was open and active in their thoughts.

Eston continued, "FLY, fly-size drones once used by prior military regimes are deployed as needed to listen and watch random conversations in public buildings. Peace Doctors programmed the FLY as a way to observe those who are likely to Flee, Lie or Yell.

Radicals who want to gain attention or challenge Goodness are well recognized by FLY."

A question was raised about Peace Doctors and Eston had to consider what they should know about a Peace Doctor's knowledge of the Goodness hierarchy. The PD was a top tier of GG's Quad and likely monitoring his work.

He didn't see it necessary to explain that the Quad was the only vertical order of authority in the world. Instead he shared, "The Quadrangle or Quad leaders manage the continents of North, South, and East & West Global Good. North: formerly North America, South: South America, East: Eur-African (Europe/Africa) and West: Ru-Asia (Russia, Asia & surviving islands). These leaders systematized the judicial and health administration teams, while coordinating the global economic development, housing and agriculture communiqué by miniaturizing what was personal tele-communication to a keycard system that interfaces with a person's microchip. This is monitored by Global Good."

The young woman asked, "How many divisions of GG are there?"

"Too many," Eston said. "There are checks and balances for all. You will have the access you need when you need it."

She realized her hand was off the scanner and blushed, quickly placing it back. He nodded at her cooperation.

Eston continued, "The northern and southern points of frozen wilderness on the globe continued to cool as global warming slowed. They house the most important vestiges of prior human history. Relics of prehistoric man, period art and artifacts from leading world religions are in the Arctic region and the archives of the Industrial revolution and the Age of Capitalism in the Antarctic. These are safe havens. Only GG leadership can access them."

Since Eston was head of the North, he was the guardian of the Arctic.

"GG determined it was important that there be a resource of past societies and governments should the new model fail. It was no easy feat moving these priceless items that represented the best of what had been *good* in previous civilizations. It took more than a hundred years to build a reliable enough labor force to handle such a delicate operation and when it was done, the museums and monuments that remained became centers of public recreation and leisure monitored by the Monument Society."

He went on to explain that the Monument Society, like other Goodness divisions, was a horizontal team-based bureaucracy. But unlike other divisions of Goodness, the Society reported directly to The Quad. The Entertainment Ministers and Peace Doctors were regulating members of the Global Good.

"The judicial court system today has term regional judge pairs and term jurors with appointed council that reviews security tapes and produces testimony within 24 hours. Anyone accused sees *justice* in a day as the evidence is recorded throughout the GG security satellites. Judge pairs are balanced with both male and female presiding and matched based on cognitive and intellectual scores. No longer would one person be the final presiding power in a trial, nor voted into office based on popularity, but rather a skilled judicial pair would reside over all matters to create a just outcome based on the governing Goodness Doctrine."

An announcement disrupted Eston's presentation. He excused himself and returned to find the eight in a circle on the floor. He watched them and caught the incoming FLY before it encircled them. He didn't want their unity broken.

"Where were we?" Eston asked.

One student waved him down to the floor. "You were talking about the Goodness Doctrine."

"Yes," Eston resumed, and remained standing. "It is based on the *respondeat superior* doctrine that historically stated an employer could be liable for their employee's actions. In past civilizations, if a slave or worker did wrong, the master or team leader would be held accountable, but in Global Goodness, every member of the team is accountable for the actions of their team. If one member of a team wrongs, the team is held responsible, as no leader or manager dominates a position of authority."

"You're an authority." The female commented.

"We are a team," Eston pointed out. "We will work together and at the moment, I am leading your instruction. But you all are Quad support. The Quad is Global Good. I am a regional Quad figurehead and you, along with multiple Goodness doctrine enforcement teams, assist me in keeping our world region a place of equality."

Eston treaded lightly on the next piece of information. "Rebels become laborers on Thirdshift."

Hands went up. Eston needed them to return to their scanpads before answering more questions. Coding would be required to equip his support with necessary data. They all got up to go to their original places in the classroom.

Eston watched as they casually moved to their chairs, jesting as they did so. He wanted camaraderie among them and not a driving seriousness.

"Meal procurements soon. If you could take your places, please." He waited until they were settled. "I know this section will invite questions, so hold them until I am finished."

He began, "Goodness leadership placed those with subpar physical and mental health in Thirdshift housing in the tunnels. Code that. Along with rebels. The parents of the physically defective are alerted of their child's unique qualities from eight weeks after conception to birth. If intrauterine surgery is unsuccessful these children are raised to work and commune where they belong, where they are wanted and needed. They have all the same benefits as the society above them: food, clothing, shelter and entertainment.

Their uniforms are white and their underground world sanitized. The goal was purification," Eston said.

He went on to explain that parents of defectives have the choice to visit their Thirdshift children monthly or move to Thirdshift and work with the infirmed and detained. Fetal and child abandonment was deemed illegal during the procreation mandate of 2070.

Goodness required that two parents join in partnership and raise their child (ren) to age fifteen. At fifteen, cohabitation in youth hostels with other teens began the transition to adulthood.

"Earlier societies that divorced, adopted or chose single parenthood were deemed self-centered codependents that raised generations of unbalanced indentured servants," Eston stressed.

"Adult children of single parents often lack good decision-making skills as their individual parent was the sole source of knowledge and thus an emotional anchor. As a child becomes an adult, role reversal sometimes emerges and the child who grew and moved on to a career, eventually has to support a parent who sacrificed to raise a child or children alone." He saw their blank expressions. He could tell they couldn't envision this. "Code that."

"History proved that the single parent martyr mentality doesn't bring about a happy, emotionally balanced, productive labor force. GG abandoned that model."

One student said, "I don't understand why one person would raise a child when partnering is much more fun and harmonious."

Eston agreed. "It's all about balance. And when the time comes, parents are not to be distracted by the hormonal changes their children encounter. Rather, Goodness makes sure that counselors, parents and the youth worked together in family activities to keep each member productive and happy. Partnering and procreation were legislated and monitored for the stability of family dynamics. The practices of marriage and divorce were abandoned."

The female wondered about emotional love and chemistry. She wanted Eston to address how that advanced from choice to GG doctrine.

"If two lovers can't find one another in daily life," Eston said, "the health administration aids those ready to find a mate. Match-makers have long assisted individuals in finding a companion with the reward of knowing these couples would someday produce no more than two healthy offspring. As needed, surrogate mothers and fathers—temporary positions inside the health administration—support same sex couples or those unable to have children. Sperm Reserves and Eggtraction were mandated to match couples to produce Good children as well as model family units."

A bell announced the meal procurements had arrived.

"To conclude," Eston clicked off the monitor. "Goodness converted the world to a place where everyone lives up to his/her potential as a workforce."

AFTER THE EGGTRACTION

9.19.2202

Sybille awaited the infirmary technician. The small and sterile patient rooms were sealed off airtight glass booths with three windowed walls and one glass door. Each contained a single cabinet with necessary supplies, an examination table and a curtain with snaps that could wrap around all four walls from ceiling to floor. Unoccupied rooms had curtains drawn.

The tech approached, held his keycard to the door and allowed the contagion reader to scan his person before entering. He did this at every booth, careful not to cross contaminate exam rooms or patients.

He stepped in carrying a long hypodermic that would settle Sybille's abdominal cramping. He also wanted to examine her eye.

"Dizziness and cramping will sometimes occur after eggtraction, but your eye twitch needs to subside or I'll have to quarantine you on the 13th floor." He was nice enough, about thirty five and dark skinned with a medium build and handsome features. She didn't care.

She was there for a follow up from her annual eggtraction she insisted and it was the first time since she began procedures at fifteen that she had ever had a complication. All women age fifteen to thirty underwent the procedure yearly as well as mandatory reproductive and gynecological exams.

ST. BLAIR: CHILDREN OF THE NIGHT

If a routine urine sample detected a woman had a rise in luteinizing hormones, signaling the ovaries were ready to release eggs, the government would bring her in for eggtraction. Her keycard would signal she had an expected appointment time and her employer would already know she was leaving early.

Sybille's vision fluttered again in the right eye. She closed her left eye and looked with her right. She saw the gold shape again.

"When did the cramping and twitching begin?" He asked.

"It's recent…" she stated.

"Before or after eggtraction?" He punched her responses into a digital file.

Sybille thought about the moment she retrieved the diary and the quake.

"After." Did it matter to anyone if the eye flutter happened before eggtraction or after? She decided it was reasonable to say it *all* happened after. What would her mother say?

"The shot will help with the cramps," he said. He gave her the injection.

She hoped she wasn't causing herself more problems, because she really didn't have cramps, but needed to get some relief for the twitch to avoid quarantine. It was the only thing she could think of that would warrant an appointment and not alarm doctors.

"Let's get you into a lightweight adjustable monocle, too."

"Monocle?"

The infirmary tech didn't have time to waste, he saw patients in fifteen minute rotations. "You'll wear it until the twitching subsides or your vision corrects. If you find you have no more symptoms just deposit it into your laundry order and it'll be recycled. If the twitch continues, you'll be held on the 13th floor for observation."

"How long do I wear it?"

"No more than a week or two."

Sybille was fitted with a stretchy black strap crossed diagonally over half her forehead and under her right ear to meet up with the thin adjustable monocle that fit closely like an eye patch. She could dial it to the lens that gave her the best vision and most comfort.

As she departed the infirmary she caught a glimpse of herself in the glass elevator. She looked like a pirate from Peter Pan. "Almost fashionable!" she muttered to herself approvingly.

BEA GONE

Sybille knocked on Bea and Frank's door. She had enjoyed dining with them and really wanted another chance to thank them. A smile crossed her face as she tapped again but it soon became a frown when her eye started to twitch. She adjusted the monocle lens as she waited.

Frank opened the door.

She knew she must look silly.

He said nothing.

"Something wrong?" she asked.

He raised his brows and slowly began in a controlled tone, "It's because of you that she's gone."

"Bea gone?"

"Yes, Sybille." He glanced into the hallway and motioned for her to come inside.

"How?"

He closed the door behind her. "Your garment was discovered in our fireplace by Joe and Anne."

"Your cohabs? How did it get in the fireplace?

"Bea put it there… hoping the embers would consume it, but instead it was discovered by Anne."

"How do you know?"

"Well Bea told me she placed the garment there and … do you understand that Goodness doesn't just take the suspect? They take the witnesses and the accusers all into custody."

She remembered what Bea said, that she wouldn't report her. Sybille wasn't sure how to react. Was she responsible for sending them all to judgment?

He motioned to the living room, Bea and Sal's photos flashed behind Frank's head. They both sat.

"She'll be fine." He put his face into his hands. "She'll probably enjoy the whole experience…" he laughed then looked up at her, "Why the monocle?"

Sybille didn't understand how he was angry one minute and laughing the next? "I have a twitch in my right eye, it's required or I'll be quarantined."

"Makes sense."

"I'm sorry." She pulled the strap off her head and placed the eyepiece on the table. Her eye started to twitch.

"Well, you don't get to be our age without looking for some excitement. Bea's a Sage Monument Guard, Sybille. She's used to bringing others to judgment. Who knows, maybe she wanted to see how the system works up close."

"I don't understand?" Her eye winked rapidly.

"Maybe you should put that back on."

"I will when I go." She placed a hand over the eye.

"Well we both knew it was only a matter of time before security would see your escapades on tape. She told me everything, including your possession of an illegal book."

Sybille was stunned.

Frank laughed in a loud burst that startled her.

"Did you put the book there?"

"No child. We wish we had known. There isn't much intrigue in this world other than in theatre." Frank patted her knee. "We've lived a long time and we find you refreshing."

"I don't understand."

"Exactly." He chuckled.

"You're laughing at me?"

He shook his head no. "You have a good heart and believe people at face value. Which is what Goodness teaches and expects, but they also want people to accept without explanation."

"But it's an offense to be cynical."

"We're taught that, Sybille. But it's human to be skeptical. We're taught to avoid questioning because the government can't control us if we find fault with their directives."

"So you're saying it's okay to question… outside of Salon?"

"I'm saying, Sybille, that you may enjoy thought-provoking topics, but the leaders of Salon will direct you back to the Goodness philosophy and that will keep you in line. That's why Salon was created in the first place."

"To keep me in line?"

"Not just you, but everyone. To keep us thinking well of others. You see it is human nature to be inquisitive, but Goodness can't hold policy or their positions of authority if citizens challenge them… so they gave us Salons, places to talk and speak freely and they LISTEN to us."

"That's a good thing, right? I mean, they'll want to take some of our ideas and help make things better, by listening."

"Well, that's one way of looking at it, but they'll also know who is highly intelligent and has potential to create a mutiny."

She put the monocle back on.

"Mutiny? I'm not really sure I understand."

"It's best to keep it that way."

"Why? How do I know what to avoid?"

"It's a rebellion and if it happens, it's not for us to know."

"But what will happen to Bea? And why does the government want us to only talk in Salons?"

"The government doesn't restrict speech; it watches for rebels. Weren't you listening?"

"Oh."

"Bea is a rebel, Sybille. I love her dearly. But she has a fighting spirit and that's why she was groomed for the Monument Society."

"What will happen to her?"

"She'll be sent to Thirdshift."

A FLY buzzed in and landed on the table. Frank squashed it.

"There's a Thirdshift?"

"That's a Salon topic that would put you on the radar," he said.

She didn't react, just watched his expression. She didn't like his tone.

"I'm not trying to insult you, child. I'm just being protective. I never had children of my own. I'm a good uncle, but…"

"Where is the Thirdshift?" She persisted, feeling offended.

"They keep the power to the city. They clean and maintain the refuse sites. They transport organ donations through the tunnel system. They are a very important part of our survival."

"Organ donations? What tunnel system?"

"You may as well know…"

Sybille's brows knitted, not quite sure what he meant.

"When a fetus or any person is in need of physical restoration the tunnel system is a channel below the hospitals that Thirdshifters use to transport organs. Its network is vast."

"How do you know?"

"The Monument Society is connected to the network. We protect the ferry boats and zeppelins, foot, subway and tunnel transportation. They are called the Thirdshift, but their society is much like our own. They have two shifts, too. They started as what used to be called a graveyard shift, but the population grew and so did their world and the need for two shifts."

"I want to work as a Monument Guard!" She was fascinated by this underground world.

"How did we go from concern for Bea and wanting to learn about tunnels to now wanting to work underground for the Monument Society?"

"It sounds exciting."

"Your skill set didn't reveal that, otherwise, you likely would have been chosen."

"Well, I want to amend my employment contract."

"You know it doesn't work like that. And, I don't think you'd actually want to be considered Thirdshift material."

"Why not?"

"Now we're getting into that gray area that may make me an accessory to your becoming a threat."

"Gray?" *THREAT?* Sybille's mind began to race from the bleak skyline to the uniform colors and she wondered if this is what he was referring to. The idea of being a threat seemed to be a thin line. How did she live this long and not question more? Why hadn't her parents ever mentioned any of this?

"Gray." Frank said in a matter-of-fact tone.

"So, how do we find Bea?"

"We don't."

"I have to get incarcerated to find her."

"You will be incarcerated, Sybille."

"What?"

"Your DNA is on the jumper. It's in evidence."

Sybille's eyes got big. She put her hand over the book in her pocket. "I have to go."

Frank nodded in agreement.

"So, you will be on Thirdshift soon, too?" Sybille asked.

"No." Frank shook his head.

"Did you turn Bea in?" Sybille persisted.

"I'm not really here."

"I don't understand?" Her eyes got big.

"Precisely." He waved his hands for her to leave.

IT'S COMPLICATED

Sybille left Frank's apartment, not certain where to go or what to do next. She looked over at the window ledge where the whole situation started and noticed it had been repainted and restored.

How was she allowed to even be in the building? Why hadn't she been detained?

It was time to read the diary in its entirety, nothing was making sense and she knew it had answers. Where to go to be alone and just read?

She heard the gnashing of the elevator as it approached the 10th floor. Her right eye began to tremble. She was paralyzed at the thought of security coming up to arrest her. She hoped it was Bea, like last time.

Sybille braced herself when she heard the loud clank announcing its landing. She waited for the sound of the metal gate to collapse its dry iron bars, but instead she saw a figure depart *through* the metal rods. A small young woman with a gold aura approached. She had dark blonde hair and was wearing a robin's egg blue stretchy shirt with a rounded neckline that showed something silver dangling from a thin metal chain around her neck. Her legs were decorated by grainy, dark blue trousers and she wore colorful shoes.

Sybille's mouth flew open and the monocled eye seemed to convulse as the girl approached. She tried to raise her left hand, but her eye was beginning to hurt.

Was this a friend or foe? There was so much to take in.

The small woman waved enthusiastically.

Sybille was impressed by the woman's bold style and she wanted to take a closer look, but why was her eye reacting so violently AND how did the girl go through the bars? Why was she smiling at Sybille? Where did her clothing come from? Who allowed…? And jewelry, no one wore jewelry unless at a gala.

"Hey." The girl called to Sybille.

"How did you do that?" Sybille asked the girl.

"Do what?"

"Go through the bars? Was that magic? I've only seen it in theatrical productions."

There was such a mix of emotions going through Sybille: fear, distraction, warmth, amazement, eye pain… The girl was a little younger than she and her shoes resembled athletic issue, but in a rainbow of checkered colors. *How beautiful!* She hadn't bothered to look up at the girl's face.

"Oh, sorry." The girl seemed to laugh at herself.

"Why are you sorry?"

"You wouldn't understand. YET."

"Yet?" Sybille repeated.

"Just go with it."

"I love your costume." Sybille's left eye was now tearing up from the strain.

"This isn't a costume. It's jeans and a t-shirt."

"AND your shoes!" Sybille was now starting to rain tears from the pained eye. She couldn't concentrate.

"Yeah, crazy sneakers, it's my thing."

"Sneakers?" Sybille couldn't take it any longer.

"Ah, shoes for running. What's wrong with your eye?" The girl asked.

"Sybille pulled the monocle off and almost immediately the particles in her right eye detached and floated to the young girl. It seemed to complete her appearance that went from hazy outline to laser clear.

The girl laughed, "I was wondering why my right hand was fuzzy."

Sybille wondered when a cohab would come out and ask her to be quiet. "What just happened?"

"I think it was from my release. It's hard to explain." The girl looked down at her right hand, surprised.

Sybille could see clearly now. "I don't understand?"

"When you pulled the diary."

"The quake... that was you?"

"Sorta."

"What are you? How can you make a building quake and go through bars and have particles float around in my eye..."

"We can discuss that another time."

"And your clothes! I love the colors in your athletic shoes. Where did you... or how did you get them?"

"I forgot... you're into fashion," the small woman said with a nod.

"What do you mean you forgot? Do you work at the Fashion Counsel, too?"

"It's complicated."

"What's complicated? Are you a cutter?" Sybille didn't interact with the workroom much.

"Ok, you're asking too many questions. I gotta go. Don't worry."

"But I don't understand?"

"You say that a lot. Just read my diary."

"Your..."

"In your pocket," she seemed a little aggravated, but then she laughed like something was funny.

"Help me!" Sybille insisted. "Why are you laughing?"

"Read! I gotta go," the small younger woman fragmented into thousands of beads of gold light.

Sybille felt a catch in her breath. It was as though time were standing still and there was no chance to say goodbye and she didn't understand why any of this was happening... Her heart raced faster. It was overwhelming: the splendor of the young woman's departure.

A gust of cold air pushed through Sybille and then a powerful sense of sadness. She really wanted to talk to the girl and didn't know what to do.

Then she realized this must be *Blair*!

YOU FOUND IT!

4.4.2001

Blair's Journal

Hi Sybille,

You found it! So glad you did. Well, I hope your name is Sybille, because that's what God brought to me. I've been on this journey for many years so it's weird to finally figure out how to do this. I guess you're wondering who I am.

It's hard to explain, but I have been blessed with vision, some might say cursed. My parents moved us to New York from Florida so I could fulfill the final leg of my mission and maybe stop the visions. I'm not dying or anything, but the mission is about your world and the earth as you know it. My mission is to place this diary where you will find it.

Anyway, I'm 17, turning 18 this summer and this all started when I was much, much younger, but I didn't understand it. I had to get help, even tried supernatural ways which I'm sure sounds very weird to you. It's just so hard to explain what you need to know so you can understand. My advisors encouraged me to complete this task as they feel my gifts will dissipate once I have fulfilled the mission. So I'm hopeful it will help you and that the haunting will end.

Anyway ...

FATE

Crystal walked through the supper club looking for an empty chair. Spotting one just a few feet from the stage, she visually seized the coveted seat. Many work friends bragged of Mancy Black's blend of jazz and unusual performance art.

Straddling a three foot wide log with shin and ankle guards, chaps, work gloves and black performance wear, the tall and brown long-haired Mancy was the picture of an intense lover. Rising and falling in rhythm with the wailing Jax Band, he stripped the timber's bark with calculating ax chisels.

Seeing him carve a trio of faces with the use of banned weapons was a rare thrill for his audience. And each performance ended with the encasing of the tools into locked metal containers which were carried off by Entertainment Ministers.

The Jax Band's two hour concert allowed Mancy time to produce a primitive totem of three new expressions nightly. Ten totems surrounded the stage this final show. Thirty inanimate spectators gawked at a packed audience. Each seemed frozen in disbelief, paralyzed by this necromantic illusionist.

Did their fate mirror society?

Could these totems remember the refreshment of being a seedling taking root in the earth's darkness and drinking in melting snow and spring showers? Could they feel the phantom branches that once outstretched to reach the morning sunlight, or commit to memory the sprouting of young leaves, the maturing of autumn's foliage?

Mancy had a rare dual talent. He began as a sculptor and designed interior works for the industrial complex in midtown. Once, during his break, he spotted a courtyard piano and sat down to play. The courtyard pianist heard his piano and feared he was being replaced. To his delight, he found the bold sculptor, a prodigy at the keys playing a bouncy ragtime tune that so inspired him that he played the other end of the keyboard. When they finished the duo drew rousing applause from the employees and Entertainment Ministers who stopped working to see their performance.

Through this courtyard discovery, Mancy was allowed to team with the pianist, now a member of the Jax Band, to periodically play the piano, but otherwise he sculpted.

The totem performance was developed after Mancy's sister Jewel suggested he elevate his sculpting to performance art. She urged him to try a new medium, wood and chisel with axes. After a trial approval and performance for the EM, Good allowed a limited engagement and closely guarded his tools.

Mancy had the rich cocoa complexion of his ancestors from Region 10. The Alliance of Nations chose to abolish prior continent and country names in the year 2150 as many had friend or foe stereotypes. City names were retained in regions where Quad leaders based their headquarters and subdistricts.

Mancy was a member of the Black Miners, a petroleum legacy started by his paternal great, great, great grandfather's family. They were oil refiners.

Crystal wished Sybille would have joined her at Mancy's performance. They had discussed it when the show posters appeared on 7th Avenue. She wasn't sure why her friend and cohab was moving in new social circles with Bea. Crystal even joined Sybille in touch therapy sessions to help her break her longing for the Nightshift boy. It was the government's recommended way to find a partner and fulfill the physical yearning for human contact.

The touch sessions were communal events for the unpartnered. Each group session included light therapy for mood modification, consensual massage of face, feet and hands whereby participants were givers and receivers, with music and aromatherapy helping the participants relax. In many sessions, relationships formed. Date centers gave couples romantic places to recline, cuddle, kiss and listen to soft music. Sex was discouraged for both disease and population control, but permitted upon partnership pledges and parenting ceremonies.

Having abolished marriage and divorce as a societal failure, the Goodness Council of 2100 needed to repopulate and incent couples to raise Good children to restore the world economy. Their procreation initiative worked too well and it became evident that parenting relations would require structure and the physical desires of the sexually promiscuous reigned in.

Crystal worried about Sybille and her private mood swings, because it seemed she could cry when they were alone and compose herself the moment there was a knock at the door. It wasn't healthy and Crystal wasn't sure how to help. But now that Sybille had new friends it forced Crystal to do the same.

"Anyone sitting here?" she mouthed to the table of five.

"You," a natural redhead with emerald green eyes mouthed back to her, pulling the chair out. "I'm Mancy's sister, Jewel."

Jewel was Mancy's surrogate sister. Their same sex parents Roberto and Clive resided in Roberto Black's residence during their childhood years. Roberto was of the Black Miner ancestry and Clive a member of Region 3. Jewel had Clive's flaming hair and ivory skin while Mancy shared his biological father's coffee and cream complexion.

Crystal slid onto the wooden seat and gazed around. All chairs were just about filled. "How did I get so lucky to have a seat up front?" She spoke into the other woman's ear.

Jewel leaned in, her mouth touching Crystal's ear, "Guess it was fate."

Crystal was excited and confused by this woman's advance. Her voice was a soft, raspy tone that only Crystal could hear among the amplified jazz.

She felt a stirring from her cheeks to her racing heart. "How about we talk after the show?" Crystal asked Jewel.

Jewel motioned a finger to her ear, then put her ear on Crystal's mouth.

"…after the show," was all Crystal could manage.

Jewel winked and closed her eyelids to listen to the wailing trumpet and intensified chopping. Crystal wondered if the other woman thought…

What did she say about fate? She certainly hadn't met anyone quite like Jewel… *Was this really happening?* She wasn't prepared to have an emotion at this time. She felt an inner smile.

Why wasn't Sybille here? She looked around to survey the mix of ages in the room. Each person seemed fully focused on the stage. A group of newly emancipated fifteen year olds gathered at two tables near the west entrance.

She remembered when she and Sybille were moved into government youth hostels. Both homesick, but fashion kept them busy. Long hours sketching, lessons in *haute couture*, examining historic fabric samples, labor intensive hand stitching of Victorian gowns and tailoring men's suits for the Counsel's Costume Closet. The girls dreamt of patterns, buttons, bows and lace. They made up silly stories about their pins, scissors and measuring tapes revolting from laborious use and attacking them in their sleep, cutting off their hair, pinning and tying them to the sheets so they couldn't move.

They and their peers were the promoters of the annual costume event and the proud creators of wearable art. Goodness knew that young people needed purpose.

Thus each child was scored with aptitude, abilities testing and physical exams from ages two to fourteen. These records were balanced with positive and negative assessment formulas to mathematically determine a ratio of success and longevity in a career. All fifteen year olds were then matched by their talent quotient and moved to selected hostels with apprentices of similar and opposite capabilities to spur creativity and community.

History proved that leaving the choice of profession and education to the immature brain was a formula for failure. Why allow disappointment in poor decision making that could lead to depression and misery? A government would never have the full resources of skilled labor if parents and children were left to decide. It was not possible to satisfy the whims of a populace and keep an economy thriving, but it was possible to help citizens find pleasure in their work by uncovering their individual gifts over peak development years. In doing so, accomplishment rose and the drudgery dropped.

Crystal couldn't keep her eyes off the danger on stage. She marveled at Mancy's talent and use of weaponry to create art and—out of nowhere—Jewel pushed her off her chair and onto the floor.

In a scream that sounded like opera, Jewel stood and sung an alarm as Crystal glanced up in time to see Mancy swing his ax at the neck of the EM stage right.

The stunned guard's eyes were clearly trying to connect with his brain when he collapsed.

The audience gasped in excitement and applause thinking this was a trick.

It soon turned to horrified weeping and vomiting as the lights went out and the chopping and screaming continued.

DEATH POSE

Crystal opened her eyes to see a uniformed figure standing over her. She caught his profile as he was talking to someone else.

"She's dead too, I believe." He kicked her ribs. The steel toe of his boot added more pain to the pounding in her head, hands and ankles. The odor of vomit was filling her nostrils and she wanted to gag but she was far too weak. She closed her eyes, not sure whether it was good to be alive.

"She doesn't look capable of this," another voice blurted from behind her.

Capable of this? It hurt to think. Her heart was racing and her mind awakening.

"She's the costume girl. Remember? You got the admiral uniform from her before." The phantom figure was a deep baritone. She figured he must be as tall as the one standing above her, but she couldn't remember anything. How did she get here? The smell of stale musty air mixed with bile was sour to the taste.

"We've moved the crowd downstairs. They'll be processed and moved to the tunnel shortly."

Tunnel?

"How many?"

"Well, not counting the bodies, about 212."

Bodies?

"When are they bringing in cleaning?"

"Why don't you just say TS? There's no one here who can hear us. They're dead or moved."

"Except her."

"She's clearly not moving."

"They have to bag the bodies, ID them, wipe the memory from their cards and round up their next of kin before we can do anything else. This place will be lights out until tomorrow."

Round up their kin? ...until tomorrow?

Crystal felt the tall man's presence lowering near her face and she instinctively held her breath, inhaling his garlic stench. He was testing her. She tried to maintain her death pose though the garlic was now mixing with the room odors and making her more nauseous.

"She's pretty." The EM said to his colleague. "I'm sorry to lose her."

"How would she return to her job?" the phantom voice in the distance moved closer.

"Well, if she couldn't remember, and she survived..."

"You're dreaming, move away. Did you feel her?"

The garlic EM touched her ribs, "She's warm." He then looked at her legs and ankles. "Looks like she was trampled... her ankles look broken."

"Wake her!"

Crystal felt herself being hoisted into stinky arms. She couldn't keep this up, her body was uncomfortably limp. She didn't want to be bagged or ... she wasn't sure.

"Ahh," was all she could manage.

"Can you stand?" He spoke softly, "I'm going to help you."

"She's not going to stand. Look at her legs." The garlic EM cradled her in his arms.

"Yes she will." The phantom EM argued. "It's instinctive. She'll stand on her own if we place her feet down."

Together they put a shoulder under each of her armpits to steady her and, once positioned, they released her. Crystal felt the collapse of her ankles as the remainder of her body followed like a building imploding. The pain shot straight to her mid skull and she was unable to catch her breath as her limbs hit the floor. Her skull bounced off the garlic EM's leg which softened her head's blow.

"I told you it wouldn't work."

All faded as Crystal's eyes pleaded with the men. The light, their voices, the dull pain, her mind. All went dark.

SHOULD I FOLLOW YOU?

Sybille entered the expansive lobby of the Fabric Counsel building. Its aged marble and gold interior appeared different today, as though she was seeing it for the first time. It was like a filter had been lifted and everything was new and transparent. She placed her right hand on the scanner and let the pin prick the heel of her palm. The reading flashed 110 and a green light came on for her to proceed. To her left another worker's light flashed red and security approached.

She could barely hear, "step into the nurse's office" over the din of bodies moving through the entryway.

This routine never seemed to be cause for concern, but now Sybille identified things differently. She glanced over her left shoulder to see the man being directed to the infirmary. She could remember a red reading once and being fed a snack. That was long ago and highly unusual for Sybille. It happened the morning after she had enjoyed a night swim. She had had trouble falling asleep and decided to go to her apartment building's indoor pool.

She would much rather have gone to the public beach and sat under the stadium lights and stars to watch the night children enjoy their recreation. She loved relaxing on the cool aluminum bleachers and looking up at the stars. She would usually lie down on the very top row, behind a neck of lights that stretched over the expanse of Manhattan Beach. The children looked like yellow fish in their bright wetsuits.

She could barely remember learning to swim, or family time at the remains of the relic that was Coney Island. All that was left were a few antique signs for the amusement park. The government closed Coney to fund a zoo expansion and give citizens a chance to see more exotic breeds, domestic animals and circus acts. The Good Bronx Zoo & Circus encompassed a carnival environment with rides and captive endangered species.

Sybille wondered if the animals had red and green readings, too. Were they tested and cared for? When she had her red reading, she had skipped breakfast. Well not exactly, she swiped her procurement keycard at the cafeteria and dumped her tray after a few bites and went on to work at the costume closet early. She desperately wanted to mend her Victorian gala gown before starting work.

She didn't feel ill at the time, just a little flush when the red reading came up, but what followed were daily visits from the health administration for nearly two weeks. They seemed very caring, a little too caring now that she thought about it.

In fact, her access at the ball *had been* restricted and she never connected it to the red reading! Why else? *Or was she imagining this?*

Crystal had been so envious during that time. Sybille had apartment visits, daily readings at work and prior to retiring for bed. It seemed the nurses wanted to make sure she was well, but now she realized … she *was* watched!

And where was Crystal now?

She couldn't wait to see her friend at the morning meeting. It would be comforting to bond again. *Should she tell her about the diary?* Would Crystal understand or would it just make life more complex for her cohab? *Look at what happened to Bea… She wouldn't let that happen to Crystal.*

As Sybille moved toward the gold plated elevator she saw a flash of something on the left door that looked tarnished. A shadow that filled the expanse in the shape of a woman's fan fluttered briefly and disappeared.

"I saw that," Sybille mumbled, as if to convince herself.

She stopped to stare as people stepped around her and went about their routine. She looked up to the right to see if the window washers or gold polishers were on the scaffolding. Something caused the shade effect and, to her surprise, the scaffolding was absent. The noise in the corridor grew louder as more workers approached the elevators, stairs and escalators to get to their workstations.

When the elevator door opened, a short white-gloved operator greeted her with a nod, "Fabric," he said. He pushed the buttons and lever as she entered.

She acknowledged him with a half smile. His short body and arms were level with the buttons and his white box hat matched his gloves. He wore the same gray as his shift. He was a greeter in symbolic garb and his head and hands were instantly recognizable in a wave.

The morning meeting commenced with a new designer, Zahndra Iyer, in Crystal's chair. Sybille couldn't ask where Crystal was, as everyone knew they were roommates and surely whatever caused the change Sybille should be privy to. And she wouldn't be able to ask. The council had rules regarding hiring, change of responsibilities and employee relations. Employees were to accept that change happens and be prepared at anytime for position modification.

Sybille and Crystal had a pact that should this ever happen they'd talk about it when they got home. They were very accepting of the idea of change as they both wanted to try different jobs at the Fabric Council.

Sybille's mind was racing. She wondered if the incident on the ledge had already put Crystal at risk? She wanted to know where she was. Was Crystal designing, sewing or … She wanted desperately to know.

When the meeting concluded, she decided to look for Crystal in other departments. She scoured the immense floors of the cutting room, sewing stations, supply room and garment closets. She didn't see Crystal anywhere and thought of Bea.

Are Crystal and Bea together?

What had she done? Where was everyone going?

"I need directions," Zahndra caught Sybille as she was moving from thread stocking.

"Oh, sorry, Zahndra," Sybille wondered if she had been following her the whole time. "You might want to head back to our offices by following the corridor …"

The young Region 25 descendant looked puzzled and started to laugh. Her thick curly locks hung just at her collar, while her aquamarine eyes and straight, perfect nose were in stark contrast with her ruddy, olive complexion and bright white smile. "No, I mean when we leave. Or just meet you at the apartment?"

"I don't understand?" Sybille was still looking at the stockers as she turned back to her fellow designer.

"I'm your new cohab."

"Of... course," Sybille knew that didn't sound right. "YOU are."

"What are you looking for?" Zahndra smiled earnestly as though she wanted to help. "I'm great at finding things."

PROCESS HER

Crystal woke to the sound of muffled voices as she blinked her eyes. She saw a low ceiling moving above her, not realizing at first that she was on a gurney, strapped down by multiple belts including the one over her mouth.

She could only move her eyes side to side to see and she smelled the garlic again and heard recognizable voices. The female sounded familiar and she wanted to lift her head but the straps restricted that thought and then she tried to wiggle her legs. The ache in her ankles shot through her whole being. She let out a guttural moan.

"She's awake," the woman said. She stopped suddenly, "I'll process her."

Process?

The velvet voice moved closer and Crystal instantly recognized Jewel's raspy laugh.

Jewel stopped the gurney and looked down at Crystal. "Aren't we in a bad state?"

Crystal's eyes widened. She felt Jewel run the back of her cold hand under her chin and up over her cheekbones. "Mancy could have taken the show down earlier, but we needed you."

She laughed. Her haunting screech echoed in the tunnel.

Only hours earlier Crystal thought she had made a connection with Jewel and now she realized she had been her pawn. This woman was the reason her body was broken, and now what?

71

Jewel's cackling laugh stabbed at Crystal's heart. She felt hot tears pour over her temples, streaming down the sides of her face as Jewel seized the gurney and took off down the hall. All Crystal could do was sob. She knew this nightmare was only beginning ...

SYBILLE'S DREAM

He appeared to Sybille, a large winged creature with the body of a man.

She could feel the heat of his body hovering over her as he spoke softly to her. The things he said were foreign and confusing. He was at least ten feet tall and, with his wings open, his shadow cast darkness over the expanse of the bedroom. The wings themselves seemed like massive exterior muscles coated in silken ivory feathers. She had only seen wings this large on an ostrich at the zoo. But a winged man?

He had thick, wavy black hair and the bluest eyes she'd ever seen. His skin was pale and his body muscular with a gold breastplate over the expanse of his chest. His torso was draped in a plush red garb and his legs were adorned in gold calf length boots.

"Most humans struggle with the concept of God, miracles and people we call saints or martyrs. These special individuals live their earthly lives in self sacrifice for God."

That word again. Like Blair's diary.

"Who is God," the winged being asked, "is God worth fighting for?"

Sybille tossed her head, trying to wake. She wanted to talk to him. It was as if he held her in stillness with his will, she couldn't move her body.

"Religious wars once persisted in the economy, the workplace, marriages, families and designated battlefields." His voice was soft yet commanding.

She couldn't turn.

"Maturing brains found evil meanings in good, deception in positives, hidden meanings, something lurking between the lines. Why? How does an innocent child trust and an adult distrust? The aging process is a series of temptation and protest. While good exists…"

Why is he mixing God and Good?

She could feel his breath, taste the scent. It was sweet like a steeped cup of brewed chai. He whispered this time, "It is a struggle to keep the mind faithful."

She held onto the thought… *keep the mind faithful*. She felt lulled, almost caressed by his tone and then abruptly he grew loud, "How does evil dominate the emotions and spread its disease inside and outside the body?"

A little overpowering.

He raised a hand to touch her and she closed her eyes, fearing a slap. He laughed.

She opened her eyes wide and stared at him, confused. *What's funny?*

He lowered his voice. "While you struggle to know yourself, there is no need… just be. Being is living."

Hot tears welled in her eyes as pictures washed through her head. She saw the ledge, Bea finding her, Blair dissolving, Frank talking, Crystal sewing, Mark smiling, her parents encouraging her at a school play. Had she lived?

"Millions are born and die and only a small quantity live. Life is not eating, sleeping and working; it is loving, Sybille."

He understands.

"Love is why God gave you life."

What is God? But how does God give life when people give birth?

She struggled again to turn and couldn't.

"Life is too hard for many. They drown in busy work that fulfills their brain's logic of what it means to live. The busy addiction separates them from love. When tragedy disables routine, busy people find another task to keep them busier and thus they trick their minds into feeling satisfied. Satisfaction is a sin of acceptance."

Sin? Tragedy disabling routine? Saints and martyrs?

She thought about Mark and how she wanted to know him. She tried to wake by counting in her head, but the winged man wouldn't allow it.

Too much information… 1, 2, 3, what is 'sin'?

"Acceptance doesn't equal understanding. Acceptance falls short of understanding and sets up a false barrier that immobilizes the need to understand."

He looked directly into her eyes, his eyes now a dark navy blue, his gaze sultry and his chiseled, flawless features muted by a gold light above the crown of his head, "Sybille, you need to embrace our message."

Our?

He knew her thoughts and he responded, "Yes, our message."

She somehow managed to lift her shoulders. Her head felt like a soapy bubble ready to pop, her brain like gelatin.

How to break his hold?

She muttered the words aloud, "our message?"

A new voice entered her auditory space, "Sybille, Sybille."

She could feel her shoulder being shoved, her body being shaken.

"It's Zahndra. You're dreaming."

Sybille turned away and put a pillow over her head.

"I want to finish…" She wanted to see the beautiful winged man but she was now conscious.

Zahndra laughed, "You can't finish a dream."

"I'm tired." Sybille tried to pull up to her elbows, but slumped back down.

"What was happening? You were talking but it sounded like OOOuuu," Zahndra took Sybille's pillow and hit her with it.

"That's not helping."

"No, but you need to wake up," the tan-skinned woman's smile was a brilliant white against soft pink lips. "We have got to mend today."

Sybille sat up, ran her fingers through her hair and yawned. "I need to mend."

"The costume ball is two months away!" Zahndra squealed.

Sybille put her hands over her ears.

"Sorry, just excited."

"I saw a costume in my dream," Sybille muttered, now inspired. She would wear wings!

"Get up. We've got work to do."

Sybille felt only profound sadness in Zahndra's happiness.

Where was Crystal? This was their joy, their favorite time of year. She heard Zahndra pad down the hall still talking but Sybille had no clue what the cheerful woman was saying. Did she even want to go to the ball?

Sybille slunk back under the covers and closed her eyes. She needed sleep and to not be tormented by creatures who talked of things she couldn't understand or visitations by a girl who could transform into light beads. Where were Bea and Crystal? Why was everyone vanishing?

Why was *she* able to still be here?

Then it hit her, Blair and the winged man both talked of *God*, but why?

Bea and Crystal were missing perhaps because of their association with Sybille. Bea was helping her, so of course she'd be arrested. ARRESTED! But Crystal?

Sybille's head and heart pulsed with anxiety. It felt wrong to allow others to pay for her mistakes. Then she remembered the term the winged man used, "Sin."

She sat up and pulled the keycard from her bedside table and typed the question.

```
What is sin?
```

She waited for a response and got her morning meal reminder, then it answered.

```
Shortened term for "to Offend a Principle"—a
literary term for "not good"
```

She thought about Frank. He would have told her not to type this, that she'd put herself on the radar again. She tossed the card reluctantly on the bedside table and saw another keycard there. Her eyes widened. She clicked the other card open.

She had entered the question into Zahndra's keycard!

SOMETHING SPECIAL
ABOUT ME

Blair's journal

My best friend is a boy named Mo. He doesn't like the name Mohammed Pasha. We have known each other since kindergarten and I call him Aladdin and he calls me Princess Jasmine. We're teenagers, but we've always liked to read aloud from kid's books and become a character. Oh, I forgot, you don't have books, except my diary. LOL (that means laugh out loud)

People think Mo and I are crazy. We hang out in the children's section of the library (a place to get books) and check-out illustrated fairy tales and folklore. You would like these, I hid some under the floor boards of my room, but I'm not sure you'll find them; the 10th floor is likely multiple rooms now. When we lived there, it was under renovation and we lived in the space near the ledge, where you found the diary.

When we came to New York, we lived in hotels for several weeks, until I could find this building. My radar, LOL, was off when we got here. Meaning the visions had to tell me where to go.

Anyway, Mo and I wanted to live in an enchanted place where people don't fight, argue or worry, where colors are vibrant, animals talk and magic is a way of life. Crazy, I know!

We ARE NOT boyfriend and girlfriend! We are 2 kids who love each other as friends and we're not afraid to say so. There are different kinds of love and the love of friends I believe goes deeper than the love of people "in love." I am guessing here, as I haven't fallen in love.

But your friends forgive you. They can hurt you and make mistakes and you still sit by them and hold their hand when they are sad. You stand up for each other in times of need and there is a kinship that is heartfelt.

Mo knows everything about me. He knows when I am cranky, when I am mad at him, when I want to eat nachos (our favorite snack) and when I am getting one of those feelings.

My mom understands, too. It has taken a long time for her to find a priest that understands me. (A priest is a religious person, more stuff to confuse you, but I'm going to get to that.) Many priests think teens are influenced by things that make them believe they are communicating with God.

Oh, and talking about God isn't well received in my day either. Everyone gets uncomfortable with this topic. So don't worry about these details, it will make sense in time.

Father Murphy, the priest, finally "got it" when he was hearing my confession April 21, 2001. (Confession is asking for forgiveness) Well, he didn't "get it" on that day, but he understood 5 months later and insisted my mother take me to a nun who is now my spiritual advisor. (Just think of the nun as a female who wants to help.)

What I said in the confessional was at the urging of an angel. Angels are winged creatures that are like God's helpers and they are <u>really</u> persuasive. Now I know it sounds crazy, but angels have been pestering me since I was a little baby.

Mom saw me in my crib talking to a very large glowing winged creature one night. It was an angel. Anyway, she was so awestruck that she passed out. When my dad found mom on the floor, he woke her and took her to the hospital. She muttered to him about the light she saw in my crib and he thought she might have an optical problem or tumor.

My mom said that night was a miracle night at the hospital. When dad wheeled mom in, I was on her lap. She said every sick person we wheeled past collapsed.

Anyway, the hospital was overwhelmed by a mass emergency that was rapidly looking like a viral epidemic. My dad wasn't sure what was going on, but he wanted his wife seen!

The next day, the paper reported a mass healing at the hospital, the likes of which science couldn't explain. Cancers, tumors, diseases, hearing and sight losses were erased, babies who were stillborn breathed. Television stations showed the security camera footage that started and ended at 9:14 p.m. from the west hallway of the first floor. In 60 seconds all cameras shut down at our entry.

A space shuttle had taken flight the same day and many thought it was an atmospheric change that coincided with the event, but it didn't happen anywhere else in the world. Mom knew it was a sign from God. (Again, I will get to God; there are many more things you need to know.)

The emergency room doctors didn't have time to see mom that night and after a two hour wait Dad brought us home.

I just started this journal because my spiritual advisor, Sister Josephine said I needed to record my life for the benefit of the future and you, Sybille.

Anyway, I guess I should describe myself. I am 5'4" and 100 lbs. I have a round head and apple cheeks, fair skin and thin brownish blonde hair. My butt is big, but the rest of me is proportioned. As for the thing I told Father Murphy, I'll write about it another time. I've got to study.

PEACE,

-Blair

BLOCK 86

Bea watched the stunned families reuniting in the holding cell in Block 86. She was bored and wanted to help, but still was uncertain what sort of event had sent the mass of people to the tunnels.

She expected some courtesy from her former colleagues; after all, she and her late husband used to process young rebels who defected from youth hostels.

Though Bea'd been out of active guard duty for more than 10 years she noticed that, while some things seemed unchanged, others seemed to be drastically different.

The maintenance of the tunnel system was near pristine. She had always marveled at how the white paint in the cavernous halls seemed to radiate brightness from the inset lighting mounted at the top arch of the tunnel ceiling. Its fresh paint smell never seemed to fade… However, she wasn't used to the intimidation process that was being used on new captives. It had always been understood this would create more altercations for those living on Thirdshift and thus a practice to be avoided.

The intention of Goodness was to correct vs. punish those being moved to the Thirdshift culture. Prisons in centuries past didn't produce rehabilitated citizens. Instead they created angry, aggressive, abused inmates who rarely contributed to the 'good' of humanity when and if they were released.

In developing the Thirdshift, the Goodness Doctrine provided that the tunnel people should live in the same team based model as the Day/Nightshifts. It required more members per team and flexibility in the Monument Society, Entertainment Ministry and Peace Doctors to work in rotation to assist in their development.

Bea had never seen such a large group of inmates in all her years as a guard. It seemed this was an insurrection that must have been carefully organized and she wondered how? She surmised that the current guards must be inept at monitoring. It seemed inconceivable that so many could have been caught in a web of deceit that brought not only a packed audience to a new existence below the city, but soon their families would be arriving.

A loud burst of laughter trilled in Bea's ears and she immediately stood to find out where it was coming from. Then she saw the gurney and the young woman on it, desperately twitching what extremities she could.

"Excuse me," Bea called.

Jewel turned and smiled at Bea. "May I help you?"

"Yes, could we speak privately?" Bea asked.

"I'm a little busy," Jewel looked down at the gurney and gave Crystal another cold stroke on her cheek.

"I see. Could I be of assistance? I am a Sage Monument Guard and I'm of no use sitting here." Bea wanted to put this exploitive woman in her place.

"Sure. I'm getting tired of pushing her around. We've got a ways to go before we get to the transplant wing under the infirmary." Bea saw many eyes look toward her and the crowds moved closer to the cell walls. Many murmured the word transplant and infirmary and their whimpering soon grew deafening.

"Quiet," Jewel shouted. She retrieved her keycard and opened the cell, letting only Bea out. All were silenced.

Crystal stretched her forehead enough to look at Bea, her eyes pleading for help.

Bea moved toward her and glanced down at the girl, her face hidden from Jewel as she gave Crystal a reassuring wink just before she took control of the gurney. Bea then tapped Crystal lightly on the shoulder, indicating that she was a friend.

Jewel skipped ahead through the tunnel, her gorgeous red hair bouncing as though she were running in a field of daisies. "Come along," Jewel screeched.

Bea kept a fast gait, but wondered who was getting the transplant? Certainly this woman would have been prepped and sedated if this were an expected procedure? Then she scanned the young woman's body and saw one of her ankles pointed in the wrong direction.

"What's your name?" Jewel shouted as she hopped along, not looking back at Bea.

"Beatrice, but most call me Bea." Bea heard her own voice echo in the passageway. She couldn't fathom how this skipping woman had been elevated to a position of guard. Thirdshift may have been created for the likes of individuals like her, but certainly not in this arrangement.

"I'm Jewel and that's Crystal on the stretcher. We needed Crystal to bring down the show."

Bea realized this was Sybille's cohab. She didn't recognize the girl in the horizontal with all the bruising.

"What show?" Bea played along. After all, she was a guard and this outrageous wild woman wasn't going to have the pleasure of shocking her.

"My brother's performance." Jewel said smugly.

"Who is your brother?"

"Mancy Black."

"The sculptor?"

"That's right." Jewel stopped and Bea almost ran her over. "Have you seen his work?"

Bea stamped both feet to a stop. "Maybe warn me when you are going to stop."

Jewel smiled. "Stop."

Bea huffed in annoyance, "I've seen his metal works in the Metropolis Museum. I prefer his early works."

"Do you?" Jewel seemed proud. She crossed her arms and cocked her head to one side as she thought. "I'm sure you'd find his final work startling."

"Final?" Bea looked down at Crystal who had the appearance of a broken doll. "What do you mean final? Is he…"

"He's fine. You'll see him shortly. We're on to bigger and better things," Jewel boasted.

"We? Are you implying that you sculpt *and* guard?" Bea knew it was impossible to have a dual career and yet this woman seemed to believe her own lies. *Typical of a Third-Shifter.*

"You'll see," Jewel mused, then approached the older woman and stroked her cheek with feigned affection. Bea gritted her teeth and held on to the gurney frame. A wave of recognition fell over her. It was an intuitive understanding and she kept her thoughts to herself.

Jewel moved to the end of the gurney and squeezed one of Crystal's big toes, "Come on, time's a wasting." Then she resumed skipping.

DREAM HOSTAGE

This time the angel Michael came to Sybille in a light sleep. He sat on the edge of her bed and restlessly crossed his legs as he spoke. His wings were tucked in and he almost looked like a normal man, with the exception of his garb and massive stature. He shared his message as though it were some prerequisite to upcoming events. She had no choice but listen, she was a dream hostage. He held her captive… his thoughts were becoming her thoughts.

He began, "I, Michael, watched over Amy Carlisle and worked for periods in human form as janitor, alongside her husband, Luke. Amy was an office manager at the cleaning supply company where Luke picked up his materials. They fell in love and were married within six months and Blair was conceived in their first month of wedded bliss.

"The pregnancy went smoothly, though we had a close call with Luke's driving. He isn't the most watchful, distracts easily, glancing too long at billboards and such, and I had my job cut out for me in the airbag deployment. Let's just say the guardians and cherubs weren't having a good day when I was done with them."

He chuckled to himself.

"So Blair arrived early and Amy and Luke went home with an alert little girl who delighted them with her gifts. It took several months for them to catch on, but Blair would signal her parents with a happy cry shortly before someone knocked or rang the doorbell. It got to a point that they would say somebody must be at the door when they heard her squeal, and then they'd laugh in amusement as someone would knock. They determined she had super hearing, though Amy began to wonder about that theory when they'd tried going to the door to test her. But they figured she knew their sounds, so they tried coaxing a neighbor to the door and she wouldn't squeal, soon they were bored and didn't continue.

"As Blair matured, her parents missed many signals. Many signals until that night—it even surprised me. Her presence in the hospital was miraculous! I had no idea of what God had in store for this child, but I knew she would do great things if we could protect her."

Michael gestured as he spoke. "There are few empaths among the billions who reside on earth. For the mathematician, roughly .000001 percent of the population are empathic and understand their Godly mission. That's not even one whole person to support Region 1 or Region 54. These aren't famous people but very plain folk, with big hearts some might say. They live in modest places and are often misunderstood."

Michael turned to face Sybille. Her eyes opened, though she still felt in a sleep state.

"You'll understand this in time. But I must continue to educate you of Blair's lineage in the context of biblical history. Of the gospel writers, only four were accepted in Christianity, so you see the job we face in numbers. There were plenty of gospels, but only those of Matthew, Mark, Luke and John are included in Holy Scripture. Our angelic order is vast and we only have a minuscule resource of humans that connect with us. Blair is one."

His wings arched a bit, like he needed a stretch. "Could that change? Yes, as we get closer to what people call the apocalypse or rapture. But these end-times events are merely self-fulfilling prophecies that humans have deemed necessary to redeem their first parents' original sin. Neither God nor his heavenly hosts require a *second coming*."

He crossed his legs the other way. "Scripture is divine in the interpretation man has written through God's inspiration. He gives his creation the ability to reason what is needed to bring them home to His Will. The peace that can exist in the world has always been. God didn't intend Free Will to be a painful journey of trial and error for his children; it is a gift that reaps happiness for those who seek happiness. It's also necessary for the continuation of humankind." He gave her a smile of reassurance.

"It might have been easier to eliminate the species as a bad experiment after Adam and Eve, but a life-giving God cherishes his handiwork and thus knows the variations in his children's talents and gifts. You'll retain most of what I'm sharing so that in time it will all make sense."

Michael was happy to be back at work in the world.

"Goodness, as your current world calls it, is a way to keep the population from thinking evil, which is a righteous practice. It began with great intention and caring."

Sybille began to close off his dialogue. It seemed sleep was beginning to dominate again. He picked up his volume and she jumped.

"The soul of a person is the intangible spirit that protects the human under attack from all enemies, Sybille. It can't be surgically removed, seen, vaporized or destroyed from outside influences. It can live on without the body, but the only way to damage the soul is for an individual to do so internally. Try to understand."

He stood and moved closer, the arch of his wings rose over his shoulders. The volume of his voice rose.

"While faith relies on something bigger than the believer, it is not something that another person can detect in those around them unless they have the gift. Blair has the gift, she is your intercessor. You may sense a person of faith, but guard against logic, instead feel it in your heart. Faith isn't a belief, it's a knowing. Thus it is between the individual and God to recognize the strength of faith."

A feather released itself from him and floated to the bedcovers.

"Blair is the Saint of Frail Souls. The frail are God's eternal children. He knows them and hopes for them and brightens the skies with brilliant sunshine and evening stars as they find and understand his love. He grieves in hurricanes, earthquakes and tsunamis for the suicidal souls lost. Many ask, 'Why would God bring the earth such awful destruction and harm?' But they never ask why the weather is so beautiful most of the time… Not that an archangel can speak for God, but I see things as a messenger confidante."

He picked up the feather and twisted it between his left thumb and index finger.

"Humans see fault with those who take their own lives and condemn their behavior as cowardly. The creator holds his children as they expire and blesses and purifies them in the fire of his love as their conscious minds have disconnected with rational thought."

Sybille felt her eyes close and warm tears wash under her eyelids.

Is this why Blair planted the diary? To stop her from jumping?

"Rest now," Michael opened his wings and departed.

ZOO DAY

It was impossible to get away from Zahndra and just think. Sybille now had the dreams of the winged man, the diary, and missing friends to sort out. The sketch pad was her only resource to just draw out her thoughts. She wished Blair would reappear and explain.

The diary was like a puzzle, but much easier to understand than the dreams and getting much more difficult to hide now that the window ledge was fully repaired.

She didn't dare enter any other searches in her keycard as she now kept Frank's caution at the top of her thoughts. Somehow Zahndra wasn't immediately endangered by the mistaken entry, but why?

The story Blair and the winged man were telling her were so different. Blair seemed like a friend who talked about how this God person directed her and the winged man was more of an authority figure representing Blair for God... if she even had that right.

And what did Frank mean when he said "I'm not really here"?

Her head was pounding and the zoo was one place she might be able to unwind and sketch for the costume ball.

She no longer wanted to go to the event, but she had no choice. She was a council member. She needed to find time to hunt for Crystal and Bea and see if Frank would help. But it would be so nice if Zahndra disappeared instead!

Sybille wasn't certain if her new cohab was just a roommate or some other mystery being. She fully expected to turn around and find the cheerful girl asking her what she was doing. A sense of defiance intensified within Sybille. It wasn't like anything she'd ever felt... and she no longer felt the desperation over a chance relationship with Mark.

In fact, he no longer consumed her thoughts. There was too much going on to even think about him. Her original anxiety over him was the catalyst of all that continued to transpire, but he was becoming a distant memory.

Instead, she was sorrowful for the friends she had put in harm's way. These people cared about her. Even Blair, a mystical being beyond anything she could ever imagine, was occupying her thoughts more than the boy who rode the subway.

It now made her angry to think of Mark. How did he not notice her or want her? It was forbidden to change shifts, but how could he not see that they would make a nice pair? She was willing to end her life for him and he didn't care! It really didn't matter that he didn't know...

Her divisive wheels were turning. She walked through the zoo entrance and placed her hand on the scanner, the green light flashed her on.

That's good, she thought. She wasn't sure if the pounding in her chest would make a difference in her reading. This gave her a more determined feeling.

She looked at the animal chart and found the ostrich icon; she nodded to one of the zoo attendants. It was dusk, she still needed to get an evening meal and she wanted to see the birds before the artificial lighting came on.

She hurried along, passing the big cats, and realized that her large sketchbook was catching a few glances. Only artists and designers had these tools and she realized she'd have to sketch her design and encode her thoughts in the pattern so as not to bring attention to herself if the Entertainment Ministers asked to review her work.

Rounding the corner to a wide pen where the ostriches were contained, she marveled at the expanse of one bird whose wings were fanning. It reminded her of the shadow she saw inside the council building. It looked like a shadow of one wing and she thought of the man in her dreams and how his wings were similar, yet very different. His were mounted behind his shoulders and these birds had them by their sides.

She began sketching a lace bodice of a Victorian gown with a small overskirt of feathers. She got excited. If the design were just right, she could remove the feathered overskirt and wear it as a cape. She would have to stitch the feathers to a broom skirt waistband with a fine gauze underskirt and leave an open seam that could fasten with a jewel button or tie with a ribbon. That way she could comfortably move it from her waist to her shoulders.

As she drew each plume, she released her pent up frustration by etching her concerns into the quilled blueprint. It gave her a realization that she, Blair, and the winged man were all communicating in a form of code; the only difference being they were speaking to her… and she was sorting out all the communications.

COSTUME BALL

After months of designing, prepping, and sewing, Sybille hoped that somehow she would find answers as to where her missing friends were, or maybe even see them.

It was evident to her that Zahndra seemed invincible. But when Sybille thought about it, she herself seemed invincible, too. It was like neither one of them were being challenged by Good, but instead were paired up for a reason, and that was beginning to bother Sybille, too.

The problem was she was actually growing fond of her new cohab. She couldn't show her any ill will or she would risk the chance of being incarcerated. Sybille's self-control was weakening. When she let her guard down, she almost felt she could trust the young woman, but something always stopped her from saying something that would give Zahndra a glimpse into her inner thoughts.

Sybille tried to act the part of a confidante with Zahndra, like she'd seen in plays. Was Zahndra doing the same? Sybille knew herself to be too transparent. She didn't have the capacity to lie, but she had learned to—out of necessity—recently.

"Hey I hope you don't mind my collar? I couldn't help but be inspired by your design," Zahndra called to Sybille from the entryway of their apartment.

Zahndra wore a black topper over the crown of her head that was embellished in blue jewels, black velvet and black lace. Her black lace bodice and blue taffeta layered gown was buttoned up to a rounded flat collar of chick feathers dyed in a similar sapphire blue as the jewels in her hat. Her small feet were booted in laced up leather socks that covered her pumps. She spun around, "Well?"

Sybille's eyes lit up, she loved the blue and the lace textures and she felt the dark colors suited Zahndra.

"What a clever shoe wrap," she marveled at the leather covers her cohab had fashioned. "You look gorgeous!" She couldn't help feeling excited. After all it was the most important day of the year. "I'm going to put on the rest of my outfit," she rushed down the hall to her room.

Sybille was wearing only an off-white sheer top with ¾ length gathered sleeves and ivory bloomers that almost touched her soft pink calf-high strapped boots. When she returned she had a thin gold band entwined in artificial baby's breath and greenery around her slightly mussed hair. The bodice of her dress was form-fitting pale pink brocade overtop the chemise undergarment. The gathered ivory muslin pull-up skirt was shorter in the front than the back and showed off her bloomers and boots.

Zahndra squealed, "Where is it?"

Sybille pulled the short pink feathered apron from behind her back and tied the beige satin bow over her skirt waistband. The feathers rested gently on the folds of her skirt and she twisted the bow behind her so the bow complimented the medium train in the back.

"I wish this day didn't have to end," Sybille smiled at her cohab. She felt flush with confidence and pride and only hoped that her friends at the council and her parents liked her design. If only Crystal, Bea and Frank could see it, too.

Zahndra curtsied. "Shall we go?" Sybille curtsied back and then in a fit of laughter, they looped their arms through each other's elbows, tucked their keycards in their bustiers and made for the door.

The costume ball was one of the few social dates hosted by the Goodness Administration that was deemed a family holiday. Sybille's parents would be there, as they were at all costume events. She wondered if Zahndra's family would also attend. It was an optional leisure event that citizens could attend and it was popular for its buffet of sweets, casseroles, meats and exotic teas. These were the only events that included a feast as all other meals were regulated by nutritional portions.

Sybille dearly loved her father Abner Malone, a hostel counselor. They shared a common passion for theatre, and she hoped they'd waltz and have a chance to talk. Her mother, Baker Fry Malone, was ever the social bee and buzzed around talking with everyone. Baker's work for Goodness Relations brought her to multiple events and job sites as she interfaced for Goodness Compliance.

The dusk sky was a darkening cornflower blue streaked with cherry pink as the city was closing into evening. Outside the civic center were a patchwork of people in a kaleidoscope of apparel clustering to be scanned prior to entry. Their noise filled several city blocks and the excitement was dazzling under the culminating darkness. Soon these night children would be dancing and making merry as their fellow citizens would in the morn.

The chilly air gave Sybille a rush of goosebumps and she decided to move the feathered apron up to her collar and wear it as a cape.

As she approached the entryway of the ball, she saw her father. In a burst of happiness, she sprinted to meet her parents.

Abner wore a gondolier costume consisting of a black and white striped shirt, straw hat, a red scarf around his neck and waist, and black pants. He was deep in conversation with a man in a toga. Baker was an Egyptian princess in black wig, gold headdress and white flowing gown with gold sandals. Sybille didn't recognize her mother at first but a familiar expression revealed the disciplinarian she knew. That look of disapproval sent Sybille to Abner, "Father!"

Abner turned and saw the feathers flowing behind her as she ran to him. "You look like a flamingo trying to fly," he laughed.

Baker didn't say a word, just looked at the cape and approached her daughter. She smiled a little weakly and just walked around the girl and gave her a once over.

"Hi Mother," Sybille looked at Baker wondering what was wrong.

"Interesting outfit, what do you call it?" Her interest was replaced by concern.

"Just something unique."

Then Sybille heard the scuffling of shoes rushing up behind her.

"I'm Zahndra," her cohab introduced herself to the Malones. Baker pursed her mouth as she observed Sybille's roommate. Baker then did the walk-around Zahndra and nodded in approval.

"The Fashion Counsel is well represented in both of you," her mother approved. "The rest of us have to checkout our costumes and you girls always get an original. Well, I'm going to appeal."

Zahndra laughed.

Sybille knew her mother's position involved conformity to Goodness standards. Baker didn't share her work with her family but if any Malone was bordering on an infraction she had only to say, "That has to go" and no questions were asked.

Zahndra jumped into position and began the first waltz with Abner.

Baker didn't notice. She was busy talking with friends.

Sybille noted her friend's boldness. Zahndra looked over at her and laughed. It wasn't a malicious look, but an expression of amusement. These moments made Sybille wonder if she was foolish, or Zahndra cunning? And yet, it was this thought process that society was to avoid…

She watched them dance, Zahndra chatting away and both of them enjoying a great deal of conversation. Sybille wanted to jump in, but figured it was best to let her cohab spill her thoughts and Sybille would inquire later. Sybille moved into position and her father nodded he'd dance with her next; the music transitioned and Abner changed partners.

"Father, what were you discussing?"

"Well, I'm sworn to secrecy," he laughed.

"We both know that's not funny."

"She really likes you. She wanted to know what games you liked to play as a child. Maybe you both could enjoy an arcade night?"

She wanted to understand my game playing? "What did you tell her?"

"The truth, you love marbles and you're a great player and shooter."

Sybille laughed. "Did she say if her parents were coming?"

"I'd expect you to know that," Abner stopped dancing and looked at his daughter. "Don't you know anything about this girl?"

Sybille took her father's hand and began leading him, but he was a little resistant. "Father, why did you stop?"

"Well, what do you young people talk about? She lives with you and works with you and you should know something about her family."

"Well, Crystal left suddenly and ..."

"You've not adjusted?" Abner was concerned. "Well, I'm sure she was promoted... you know these things."

"But I never believed it would happen."

Abner squeezed his daughter's hand and Sybille felt tears of tension fill her eyes.

"How about we grab some tea," Abner directed her off the dance floor and no sooner had they moved toward the beverage buffet than Zahndra looped an arm between them and they became a trio.

"Where are your parents Zahndra? I'd like to meet them." Abner gave Sybille a knowing look, which Zahndra caught immediately.

"Mother had eyelid surgery and father is with her."

Sybille didn't believe her. It was common practice for elders to have drooping lids lifted, but Sybille felt this was an excuse.

"My parents work with your wife in Goodness Relations," the young woman seemed proud.

Now Sybille really felt awkward.

"Give them our best," Abner said. "What are their names?"

"Ira and Raja Iyer."

"Well I'll ask Baker if she knows Ira and Raja. We could dine together sometime."

Sybille watched as Zahndra smiled really big, then excused herself and moved toward the dance floor.

"Let's enjoy some tea and cakes," Abner suggested as he drew tea for each of them from a silver service. Hundreds of teapots were set up on multi-tiered rotating platforms that provided guests with an opportunity to have a fully steeped cup of choice tea. The main course was a spread of samplers from rabbit pie to rice rolls, petite sandwiches, star-shaped fruits, casserole cups, soup tubes, cake bites, mini tarts and pastries.

Taking it all in was enough to sway Sybille's thoughts for the moment. She agreed with her father, "Tea and cakes sound perfect."

Sybille had danced for a full hour with counsel friends while also keeping close tabs on her parents. She didn't want them to leave without saying goodbye.

A young man drew close to her. His makeup was reminiscent of a raccoon, with black bands around his eyes and a patch of black at the tip of his nose. White makeup in swatches above and between his eyes separated the black bands and his drawn gray whiskers accentuated a naughty grin. His black hair was spiked up with gray grease paint and he wore a set of faux fur black ears and a form fitting waistcoat of grayish white with a black cummerbund over his flecked gray trousers. Attached to the clip of his cummerbund was a fluffy tail of black rings over tan.

He had a swagger that was intense and theatrical. She couldn't help feeling a rush of excitement as he approached her.

"May I have this dance," he bowed to Sybille. As he rose his eyes fixed on hers.

These eyes were familiar and she wanted to be polite as her voice quavered. "Do I know you?"

"Know?" He thought out loud.

"Oh, I didn't think so," Sybille replied shyly.

His charisma was powerful. She mused at the choice of costume. A furred bandit.

He laughed.

"Did I say something funny?"

"Yes." His white cubed teeth glimmered as he smiled wide and his demeanor changed to playful.

Then it hit her, like the time she saw Blair exit through the elevator for the first time. It was obvious, but she didn't believe what she'd seen. She looked into his eyes, the aquamarine was the same, the mouth the same and yet, there was no possible way.

"We've seen each other in passing," he said almost casually.

Her heart was racing and her eyes filled with tears. She wanted to hug him, kiss him and yet she was frightened. *How could he be at her event?* Maybe there was some hope, some way for citizens to move between the shifts?

Did he actually seek her out? Did he feel the same for her? A million thoughts were racing through her mind and her whole being was tingling with a heightened awareness she had never experienced before.

"Shall we dance?" He extended his hand.

Sybille reached out and held his hand and they walked toward the swirling of costumed dancers moving to the quickstep.

She wanted to wait but before she knew it, they were among the crowd. She felt as though she were chasing him even as they ran side by side. They were locked in hold, moving faster from one end of the dance floor to the other. There was no time to talk. She wanted to match his skill. Both breathed hard in the rush of the dance. They couldn't speak, just smiled at one another and moved rapidly with the melody.

This had to be Mark, it could only be him.

She was hoping her parents were watching. She wanted them to see this chemistry and magic. The excitement of being in his embrace was dizzying. Together they moved in perfect time, locked together.

He sought this connection. *He* initiated the dance and now *he* had her in *his* grasp.

Her cape flew out behind her in the cadence of the dance and she felt as though the feathers would become the wings of her escape. Perhaps she could take them both from this place in her flight.

When the music stopped they were both breathing hard and smiling, but not able to speak.

His makeup was glistening and beginning to streak. His hair looked like morning dew on charred grass.

They walked together to a table lined with crystal pitchers of water. He poured her goblet first and then gulped one himself. She picked up a linen napkin and dabbed his black makeup.

"I don't want your mask to run," she laughed.

He didn't seem to mind. His eyes closed as she tended to him.

It became an intimate moment. They could feel each other's warm breath, panting from exhaustion. She took her time repairing the makeup and when she was finished she reveled in the blue gems gazing back at her through the dark greasepaint.

"Please tell me your name," Sybille asked.

"You don't recognize me?"

"I fear I do, that is why I ask."

"Why do you fear?"

"Because you aren't supposed to be here," she whispered.

A rush of images raced through her mind: the view downward from the ledge, Frank saying he wasn't there, Blair dissolving into beads of light, the winged man, typing in Zahndra's keycard, her mother's *scrutiny…* and then *him. Here…*

Suddenly she realized this handsome creature had been answering her.

He laughed, "You've not heard a word, have you?"

She shook her head to confirm that she wasn't paying attention.

"It's just as well," he took her hand and kissed it. A black smudge from his nose dotted the heart line in her palm.

She really wanted to cry now. "I'm sorry. Could we start over?"

"I'm afraid I have to get back to my work," he said.

"I'm Sybille, and you?"

"A raccoon," he bowed.

"Will we see each other again? Could we meet?"

"Perhaps," he said.

Sybille felt a tap on the shoulder and was ready to strike whoever it was, especially if it was Zahndra.

"Baby, we are heading home," Abner kissed the top of her head. Sybille was relieved.

Abner extended his hand to Sybille's dance partner. "Abner Malone and you are?"

"Marcus Boucher, sir."

"Please meet Sybille's mother, Baker." Abner stepped back to give Marcus a chance to greet Baker.

Baker looked directly at Marcus then around the room.

"Hello," she said in a slightly annoyed tone.

Sybille watched her mother's demeanor. It felt like there was some familiarity between Baker and Marcus, and it seemed Abner was oblivious to it.

"If you'll excuse me," Marcus addressed the trio, and then departed.

Sybille wanted to chase after him but there was something unsettling about his behavior.

Her mother gave her a long hard stare.

"Mother, you know Marcus, don't you?"

Baker laughed mockingly, "Well, who don't I know? Really, Sybille."

No Promises

Blair entered the room much the same way she had departed on their first meeting. She walked through the door of Sybille's bedroom in beads of golden light that formed into a full person.

"Hi Sybille, did you read the diary?"

Sybille was looking down at her keycard screen when she heard the voice.

"Blair!" She was startled but happy. "Don't leave like you did last time. I need to talk with you."

"No promises, Sybille." Blair laughed.

"Why do you laugh so much?" Sybille looked at her, puzzled.

"Is that what you want to know?"

"No. Just don't leave suddenly. I need to know about the diary and the dreams and why everyone is disappearing."

Just then Zahndra knocked at the door and Sybille's eyes got big. She mouthed to Blair, "Don't do it."

And Blair began to de-crystallize while smiling at her. She mouthed at Sybille, "I'm coming back."

Zahndra opened the door and said, "Were you calling me?"

"No," Sybille replied.

"Were you talking to someone?"

"No," Sybille repeated.

"Then what were you doing?"

"I like to think aloud."

"Me too." Zahndra came in and sat on the bed.

"Alone," Sybille clarified.

"Why?"

"It's just a preference. Do I have to explain everything, Zahndra?"

"Well, we are getting to know each other."

"Give it some time. Crystal and I were cohabs since hostel, I can't just pick up with you like I've known you forever. "

Zahndra reached over and put her hand on Sybille's. "I do understand, but we're having fun aren't we?"

Sybille didn't appreciate the gesture, she wanted to slap her hand, but instead she just sat there. Zahndra understood the silence and got up.

"Ok." Zahndra said. "But I know we'll be great friends."

Sybille couldn't sleep and stayed awake waiting for Blair. She pulled out the diary from the floorboard under her garment cube. It was a weak spot in the floor that always creaked and once she had no place to go with the book, it was the only place she could maneuver to hide the item. She began to reread parts.

> ... Then Josephine lit a candle on the table between us. She is a nun in her early forties and wears no makeup or habit (it's a headpiece that religious women wear). Her uniform is a white blouse under a tan jumper and beige flat sandals. She's kinda plain with a boyish look.

Sybille suddenly realized the attire sounded much like what she wore day to day, very basic.

> Her hair is short, dry and brown... in need of conditioning! Her scalp snows flakes on her right shoulder strap more than her left. Hard to believe,

but she was a big time marketing executive before she became a nun.

Anyway, Sister Josephine is a modern nun. A nun is like a religious job for women. She didn't have much life outside of work when she was an executive. She told me she was faithful to her job and God and she didn't take time to build friendships... and forget boyfriends! She went to mass on Sundays and penance (like something you do to make up for bad things) twice a year for the sins of her company, she said. She didn't agree with her bosses and she became what they call a whistleblower (which is someone who tells the truth about a bad situation that is being ignored).

Sybille stopped at this part. She was thinking about the term whistleblower and it resonated with her. She wanted to blow a whistle in Zahndra's ear! And blow one that brought answers to all the questions she had, and she wanted to blow one to get Blair back!

It cost her.

Before she became a Sister or nun, she said she turned to God for strength. She said she was a lost soul with no connections, no shoulder to cry on, and no one to love, nothing. A slave to her job, she always ate lunch alone while working, and watched movies at home and worked on her laptop. She never even decorated her condo (which is another name for apartment), as she traveled the world 80% of the time for work.

Sybille wondered how anyone got permission to travel outside of the city. She also wondered how Josephine was able to live alone with no cohab.

OK, you'll like this. She told me her closet was a mini boutique with a vanity, makeup station, organized suits and running clothes. Shelves of shoes, briefcases, handbags, belts and scarves, with costume jewelry filling several display cases to compliment the colors of her wardrobe.

Anyway, she was emotionally crushed when she was fired from her job for blowing the whistle on her bosses. Her bosses were reporting false information about the company and she was supposed to ignore it, but she didn't.

When she lost her job, she had plenty of money saved, but no friends. She struggled to find purpose in her life. Her faith brought her to work with the homeless (something you don't have in your world. They are people who live in the streets and they are dirty and hungry).

Sybille couldn't imagine people living in the streets. And no food? Weren't they allowed to go to the cafes and get their procurements? There wasn't much space on the streets with all the foot, bicycle and bus traffic.

So she let a bunch of homeless people live in her condo with her.

Sybille thought it was funny that a condo was an apartment, and she wondered if condo was also a word for cohabs? Blair's terms weren't always clear.

Up to forty people moved in with Sister and she got kicked out, because it was against the rules. It seemed that no matter what good she did, she was rejected.

Sybille couldn't imagine forty cohabs in one apartment… and how does someone get kicked out? She wondered if this was a primitive punishment.

Sister Jo then moved to the streets with 'her people.' It was bold and insane, Bishop Wright said. (A bishop is an important religious job that men do).

She could have bought several apartment complexes and moved the poor into them, but she wanted to be one of them? I mean I think she is really great, but I like to take a bath and watch TV and eat good food.

Sybille marveled at the thought of buying her apartment complex. How did anyone get permission to do this? She wondered what the woman's procurement allowed. And her different jobs? It was so exciting to think about. She wondered about TV.

It's not like she didn't have the intelligence to educate, tutor and assist them in legal stuff, but she wanted to see the world from their eyes, she said. She lived under the expressway with mostly men to begin with, and encouraged the women to move into shelters (a group home for homeless people).

She was never harmed, but she did panhandle with them (which is begging for money and she had money!). She said she often kissed the hands of the givers, which didn't go over well sometimes.

All the while her bank accounts grew and her investments tripled. She was a very wealthy woman living in squalor.

Sybille wished Blair were there to explain what a bank account and investments were.

Bishop Wright tracked down Sister Jo after a year of hearing stories from parishioners. He spent an evening in prayer (it's a form of meditation) with her and her companions under the I-75 off ramp.

Sybille liked meditation. She might try an evening in "prayer."

So she said Bishop Wright asked her, "How does God want you to steward your blessings? Eating garbage and starving might seem like an act of piety, but your body is a temple," he pointed to his chest to infer the body she told me, "It is physically being destroyed in this heat. As a temple of the Holy Spirit (hard to explain), how do you fulfill the call of Jesus (you won't understand yet, but Jesus is God's son)? Come off the streets, work in the free Clinic and see what health and wellness look like for the poor who get real help."

Sybille liked thinking of her body as a temple. She liked meditating in Temple Good. If she were a temple of meditation, she would like to have colorful candles inside, instead of the clear wax that liquefied in the large candle pots in the temple's square. Candles were considered a focal point for the meditation and each meditation participant communed with their fellow citizens in fifteen minute rotations.

Josephine said the bishop looked at the homeless men she lived with on the streets... most were passed out and reeked of urine and alcohol.

"If they were willing, you could afford to put them through rehab, Jo. Do you consider these people your family?" Bishop asked her.

He also wanted her to regain some strength before she'd be too weak to reason with. She told him that the beneficiary for her assets (all the stuff she owned) hadn't been declared. He feared she'd die and the state would take her money and waste it. He knew how much she wanted to help women rise above poverty and he wanted her to open a foundation and find her calling.

It took more than two years of Jo living on the streets to bring her back to reality. She knew money didn't make her happy, but she did eventually reconnect with her ailing grandparents and distant cousins. She gifted money to them and donated the remainder to food banks before joining the Sisters of Mercy order. (A group of nuns)

Sybille liked the term 'Sisters of Mercy.' She hadn't thought about what mercy might really mean. She knew it had something to do with being understanding.

Since many of the homeless she lived with converted to the faith, the bishop recommended she work as a spiritual director. Her amazing insight into supernatural gifts and her visions of St. Michael the Archangel became well known.

Michael? Why does he talk to me in my dreams? But Blair called it visions, and I have visions of Blair...

When Sister Jo met me, she said she felt the presence of one who had the gift of prophecy. I shared my frustrations with the premonitions (well I called them post-monitions at the time, LOL) and absorbing the pain of others (we haven't gotten to that yet). It fascinated Jo. She said she could feel frustration in my body language.

It took awhile for me to get comfortable sharing with her. Many times I told her I didn't want to come back. And then something would happen and I knew I was supposed to discuss it with her.

I wanted to be normal like other teens. Instead, my "gifts" were a magnet to my troubled peers and other supernatural beings. It was emotionally draining. They all wanted to tell me their darkest secrets and being an "instrument" of faith, I couldn't ignore them. I had to help them.

One day I asked her, "Why do you have that picture of Michael?" It was hanging in her office.

Wish I could see it, I'm sure that's the same Michael who keeps pestering me, Sybille laughed to herself.

Josephine looked into my eyes and said, "You know him well, don't you?"

I'm beginning to, Sybille thought.

I didn't speak, but it was great to know she understood. We didn't have to talk after that. We both knew Michael and it was just something we didn't talk about. That's when she said, "Start a diary. If you read the lives of most saints, they journal and write what God shares with them. It will give you peace, she said. (It's hard to explain, but Michael is not only an archangel, but he's a saint, too. There are only 3 angels that are named in Holy Scripture and each is considered a saint. Otherwise, saints are people).

Saints? Michael used that term with her, too. But she wondered why he didn't think of himself as a saint?

Sister Jo asked me if I would journal and, you know the answer.

Ok, but I need you to reappear, Blair!

CRYSTAL AND BEA

Bea removed the binding that held Crystal to the gurney. Crystal whispered, "Thank you," as a fresh stream of tears poured from her eyes.

Bea shook her head, meaning this wasn't the time to show weakness.

Mancy approached the pair of women and seemed almost embarrassed at Crystal's injuries, but he quickly changed his stance when his sister Jewel walked toward him.

The room was a surgical ward and they awaited the surgeon's diagnosis. Only moments prior Jewel had explained to the Peace Doctors the events that brought Crystal to this condition. Mancy had performed with his band and carved totems throughout the set. An Entertainment Minister and his cronies took matters into their own hands and struck out at the audience with Mancy's tools. Crystal was the only survivor.

Crystal knew it was a lie, and remembered Mancy whacking the EM with his ax, but didn't dare mention anything. She was hoping Bea would still help her as she was certain Jewel had a plan to harm her.

"Will I be able to return to my work at the Fashion Counsel once I am healed?" Crystal asked. She knew the answer, but had to confirm it in order to condition her mind for change.

Jewel laughed. "Really Crystal? Ya think so?"

Bea grit her teeth and hoped Crystal could do the same.

Crystal became indignant, "I figure if you can go back and forth, there must be a way?"

Bea wished young people had more control and didn't react so quickly. She knew Jewel was baiting her.

Jewel laughed hysterically. But the surgeons didn't seem to take offense or even notice Jewel's behavior.

"Why did you say you needed me to take down the show?" Crystal figured she had nothing to lose at this point.

Jewel bent over and placed her mouth on Crystal's ear, much the same as she did in the club, "Let's say we need your connections. I'd refrain from speaking if I were you."

The surgeons interrupted them and reassured Crystal that they would be able to set both ankles and inject her own fortified bone marrow back into each ankle to speed up healing. She wouldn't be able to walk much right away, but could go to work mending garments in the Thirdshift laundry, since she was an experienced designer and seamstress.

Crystal wondered if Sybille had any idea what was going on.

Bea thought for a moment and turned to the doctors, "Who will care for Crystal?"

They all seemed dumbfounded by the question.

"We will," one finally said. "She's our patient. Why do you ask?"

Jewel crossed her arms and cocked her head to the left and just watched Bea.

"Wonderful," Bea said.

Crystal seemed more relieved, but there was still a huge weight hanging in the air.

The surgical team, satisfied they had answered all questions, began to move about, prepping and scrubbing at adjacent sinks.

Bea wondered when she and Jewel would be excused, as surely they would now begin to get Crystal cleaned up for the procedure.

"You can leave," Jewel said. "You have to go back to the Block."

"We'll go together then," Bea was firm.

Jewel grinned, "I don't think so. I'm Crystal's nurse."

MICHAEL PREPARES
FOR BATTLE

Sybille tossed and turned in a restless sleep.
Michael took hold of her dream and conveyed the following, which would lay dormant in her subconscious:

> *The serpent in the garden was only the beginning. He was once filled with divine goodness and a member of the legion of angels, but the demon drank his first taste of blood in the death of Abel, the keeper of the sheep, by the hand of his brother Cain, a tiller of the land. The serpent's temptation brought about the first sin to the first parents Adam and Eve and the first children Cain and Abel.*
>
> *Could the offspring of parents who ate of the forbidden fruit of the tree of knowledge tend the flock, till the land and sow seeds of love? It was the death of the first shepherd Abel who brought about the coming of the Lamb of God, Jesus.*
>
> *The line of Abel, had he lived, could have brought about peace and prosperity to Eden and restored God's trust in his creation, but instead the stain of original sin would not be erased, nor paradise restored. Abel did not escape the wrath of Cain's jealousy for the disease of envy reared its head and struck him in his early years. The descendents of Abel might have carried on a family dynasty of harmony and order had they*

the right to exist, but instead many prophets and holy people would be summoned and many centuries would pass before a messiah was called to save a people who couldn't maintain a relationship with their creator.

The cycle of despair, dependence, hope, abundant blessings, comfort, laziness, and separation occurs with each generation. Jesus, as God in human form, would shepherd 12 apostles to carry on his mission of love for believers and unbelievers in an effort to call all to a new paradise. The hope cycle didn't stop with Jesus, but it did add a new element: faith. Faith in a resurrected savior who would come again in the end times and bring all home to heaven.

His disciples weakened and in time Saul was called to revive their beliefs. A zealot Jew and slayer of Christians, Saul was blinded by the light of Jesus' love on the road to Damascus and given a new name, Paul. Paul was given back his sight and called to bring many to the faith. He did good works and educated many.

The demons we slay today are born of intelligence and the human psyche. Their motives are selfish and controlling, their clever reasoning spin. I overheard a demon rationalizing that if a human happened to die as a result of a sequence of events the demon had started, it wouldn't be the demon's fault, because the chain could be broken at some point through the human's free will. The elaborate plot had many twists and it would take a diabolical mind to follow the progression. Do demons really believe they haven't an opposite? A brilliant mastermind who is an agent of love?

I, Michael, have been created as an instrument of God's devotion to humankind. He instructs me to guard and protect His children. I do not enjoy the battlefield, yet I must fight. I will not allow evil to win. I wage war on those who prey on the holy and I will slay them in the name of God. It defies my *mission of peace and security, but it is the last defense. I do not want to strike down a child of God or even a demon who once was my angelic brethren... but I cannot leave the innocent open to attack! No!*

The slaughter of any being cannot be reconciled as an act of love which is the dichotomy of my mission. Hate knows no enemy. Hate is negative energy. Cain abhorred Abel and eliminated him.

Could Abel have stopped Cain's blind insanity with a display of kindness?

Perhaps if Abel knew he was going to be attacked he might have reasoned with his brother, but a victim who is blindsided doesn't have a chance to react in love.

Can I be emancipated from the acts of brutality I must inflict to shield the innocent?

My adversary learns from his environment. I wouldn't have to fight if he understood affection, kindness and charity. He wouldn't maintain an attitude of hatred if he embraced compassion, benevolence and gentleness. Can demons be rehabilitated?

Yet time passes and centuries of devastation have brought us to this place where God has let the people attempt heaven on earth and Goodwill toward men. He hoped for the best but sent a Saint ahead to communicate for salvation's sake.

While Eve tempted the first man Adam, one of her millions of great granddaughters will bring closure to her mistake.

I am preparing for battle today. I bow before the one I will defend. It is my honor to serve God and guard the soul who is under siege. It is my hope that my opponent will surrender or flee and I will not have to resort to bloodshed.

May God's will be done.

GOOD RELATIONS

Baker sat across from Marcus Boucher and asked him point-edly, "Why are you targeting my daughter?"

Marcus stared out the window, barely listening.

The view was amazing. The 82nd floor window framed a canvas of white billowing clouds against a crisp blue backdrop. The Fifth Avenue Sky Tower was an historic landmark in prior civilizations. The ancient building was among seven worldwide designated Good Relations Sending Stations for keycard readers and linked to a main satellite that geostationarily orbited the earth.

"Well, to be honest, she is quite attractive and she has been flirting with me on the subway. She knows better and she said as much on the dance floor." Marcus uncrossed his legs and folded his arms, smirking at Baker.

"And we both know entrapment is illegal," Baker snipped.

"But we're a team, Baker. We back each other up."

A small drone hummed in the background and entered the room through a wide air conditioner vent. The small bug entered their office and flew between them. Marcus reached up and grabbed it, looking right into the mechanical bug's eyes as he spoke.

"Nice try, guys. Find some real problems to investigate," he tossed the drone into the air and it buzzed back around Marcus' head and out the same vent from which it had entered.

"So that means we all go to Thirdshift, Mark?" Baker snapped.

"We'll be one big happy family," he laughed.

"Seriously, what's your point?" Baker was growing impatient.

"Baker, do you love your daughter?"

"Are you threatening me?"

"I want to understand your mother/daughter bond."

Baker looked at him and didn't respond.

"Okay, I get it. You're being protective. But I've got to hand it to you, Sybille is very naïve. You've obviously never shared your work with her because she doesn't know about us."

Baker glared at him.

"I mean, I don't know how the average citizen doesn't realize we drift between the shifts? How else do we keep our partners honest?"

Baker placed both palms down on the glass top table and stood. "You've been following Sybille for months, I've reviewed your activities … and now you are playing with her emotions. What do you want from her?"

Marcus leaned back and laced the fingers of both hands together behind his head.

"It's not what I want from her. It's what I want from you." He smirked.

NO PLACE LIKE HOME

Blair's journal

OK, the weirdest thing EVER happened yesterday. Just remember that it was a bright sunny day and not a chance of rain. I can't explain it. I was meeting with Sister Jo a week ago, she is now helping the youth ministry with a retreat and she asked me to witness at mass, to help recruit more teens to sign up.

Well, I had a paper to read from, because Father Murphy doesn't want teens to talk at mass if they don't have an outline. Spoiler: it didn't go as planned.

Let's just say, the spirit moved me!

It was Paul, to be exact. He was a famous apostle who spoke to the churches in Corinth, Galatia, Ephesus, etc.

Well, I got up to do my witness and I had the paper with me and it was like a time warp happened, or something. Mo was sitting with my parents. The closer I got to the podium, I felt kinda like I was going to pass out. I wasn't nervous. Really, I WASN'T. But I wasn't in control from the time I got near the altar, approaching the podium.

It was like something passed through me.

I looked at everyone; the church was full at 8 am. This was the first mass I was to speak at. We have 4 masses on Sunday and I was to be at each. The 8 am was the family mass and afterwards a full pancake breakfast was served, so I was already thinking about the butter and syrup and when I opened my mouth to speak it began: "Grace to you and peace from God our Father and the Lord Jesus Christ."

I looked at the paper and that wasn't written down and I spoke again: "Brethren, by the name of our Lord Jesus Christ, I warn you that a storm is coming."

I looked at the crowd and I could see confused looks and Mo was smiling, like **you go. girl.**

"A storm that will cause division among you and yours. Many who have much will lose their homes and become poor. The poor will be lifted up and exalted in due time. But the storm has been brewing and you are in the eye of the storm now. Please open your hearts and homes to those who are suffering that you may not suffer."

Father Murphy jogged over and slapped his hand on the microphone and it made that loud squeal. Everyone was making that "huh" sound. This kinda snapped me out of the moment. He pulled the microphone to himself and said. "Thank you Blair. Not sure what that was about, but our youth are very theatrical. Her message was supposed to invite the youth on a Summer Retreat, so all teens ages 14 and up please sign up in fellowshi..."

Then a sudden clap of thunder shut the microphone and the electric off before he could finish. Father was irritated, but the parishioners were looking up at the skylight that went black as a storm began at that moment.

It was a sunny day, like I said, and it turned into tornado weather rapidly. Father was talking as loud as he could, but he couldn't be heard over the hail that rained down on the skylight and pelted the windows. His anger totally distracted him.

Father nudged me away and I was really glad to move on, but I knew this wasn't going to be the end of Paul. The parishioners were muttering, "Let the girl speak, can't you see what's happening. We're in a storm!"

But Father was determined to continue services and ran to the back of the building to get the backup generator on and people were talking loudly amongst themselves and the noise level in the church was growing. Some were worried if we were having a tornado or something. When Father returned, people were standing and encircling me, asking me questions. Father asked everyone to join in the prayers of the faithful, which got mixed groans.

I had to pee by then and I crept out and just stayed in the bathroom until mass was over. The rain made for a long departure for many and what I didn't know was everyone was looking for me. When I eventually came out of the bathroom Father, my parents, Mo and some of the elders were waiting. I opened the bathroom door to a crowd.

"What prompted that, Blair?" Father asked.

"I don't know," I said.

One man said, "That sounded like St. Paul's writing."

I said, "Yeah, Paul."

Father said, "Yeah, Paul. What does that mean?"

"OK, it was Paul."

My mother jumped in between all of us and just grabbed my hand. "It's time to go." She knew this wasn't the time to discuss my spiritual encounters. She, Dad and Mo were the only ones who understood. My dad used to think it was just was my imagination, because he had a difficult time embracing these events.

Father Murphy stopped mom. "Let's finish this."

Everyone stood there staring at me. I knew this was my chance to get it over with.

"We're going to experience a worldwide famine in the future, that's what Paul wanted you to know."

Father rolled his eyes. An elderly visiting nun, small and frail like Mother Theresa grabbed my hand and asked me if I pray the Divine Mercy chaplet for those who will suffer.

"I do, sister. Do you know Saint Faustina?"

She closed her eyes, dropped to her knees and began the **Our Father**. Then everyone was on their knees saying it and I passed out.

When I woke up I was in the church office and I felt like Dorothy in the Wizard of Oz (at the end) looking at familiar faces. I understood the theme of that movie too well: <u>I really wanted to go home!</u> But instead I had paramedics checking me. They found nothing wrong, but asked if I would go with them to the hospital to make sure I was okay. All I could think was: I am never going to live this down. Father will always have his eye on me! But I guess that is what God wants, some way to get Father Murphy's attention.

Peace,

Blair

TUNNEL CULTURE

Bea stayed on with Crystal for as long as Jewel would tolerate. There wasn't much time during the Peace Doctors prep. Jewel had to get into her scrubs, so Bea figured she may as well educate Crystal about Thirdshift, as she didn't know what might happen next.

The mild sedative was beginning to quell Crystal's anxiety and her grasp on Bea's hand. Bea began in a close whispered tone.

She explained as if telling a bedtime story that Thirdshift started as one day part at its inception and, as their population grew, it had developed into two unique shifts like its surface counterparts. These were designated A and B, or better known as TSA, and TSB.

The term Thirdshift began as a way of distinguishing 3 separate groups of society, two above ground and a third below. But they were also known as *tunnel people* in earlier days, until Good Relations deactivated that term because they favored the nondescript as a way of managing the populace and not showing preferential treatment.

Each group had to manage their incoming and outgoing food production, maintain their shelter, police their people and grow the industries that sustained their shift—and do so with the support of Good Relations, Peace Doctors and the Entertainment Ministry.

The Health Counsel handled the transportation of organs, blood supply, and critical medical necessities, including perishable foods. All were kept in the cool confines of the tunnels for all shifts. The movement of items from below to above ground was made possible through industrial elevators that were loaded and timed for unpacking by Day or Nightshift crews. Workers were conditioned to believe that lights-out robotics moved the items onto the elevators through keycard procurement.

Computer systems were used to send and receive the orders. The crews on each shift, surface and below, loaded the supplies on the elevators, though they didn't know it was humans doing the fulfilling. They believed robotics gave them their order fulfillment from storage. Only Good Relations knew what the total supply was for their region and made adjustments or increased production through the management of the Counsel of Commodities.

The surface and tunnel societies sent supplies up or down for storage and use from the same elevators. Rebels who were removed from the surface society to the tunnel were reprogrammed in Block 86 in an effort to keep them from inciting chaos below.

The tunnel people weren't permitted to live above, and only designated surface parents whose children had been born with irreparable birth defects could go between the surface and tunnel culture. This *societal forgiveness* was deemed Good's answer to an irreversible genetic defect and the visitation practice referred to as *Twinning*.

Prior antiquated universal healthcare systems that once gave individuals modest choice was replaced by a true worldwide health ministry that trimmed the fat of unhealthy lifestyles to a lean, mean, productive machine in the form of Goodness Knows.

Goodness Knows was the first adaptation of universal wellness and the oversight committee for the Health Counsel that revived the remnants of the Bacterial Plague. With the current population's expanded longevity and improved physical and emotional health, it was naïve for Goodness leaders to continue the practice of *Twinning*, as this truly made Twinner parents elite.

No doctor wanted to deliver a defective. Genetic testing and fetal surgeries were to be performed to avoid such. If, after all was done, a Peace Doctor delivered a defective child, the parents had the privilege of choosing: a move to Thirdshift with their offspring and building their family life below, or *Twinning*.

Twinning was for a limited time, but the parents weren't informed.

Twinning was Goodness Knows' way of challenging their doctors to achieve genetic excellence. And the GoodEgg bank destroyed Twinners' eggs and sperm to avoid more defectives.

When a defective turned fourteen, their parents (the Twinners) were no longer able to move between the surface and tunnel. The defective graduated to the Thirdshift youth hostel and the Twinners (without warning) would be moved below permanently and reprogrammed for transition to avoid rebellion. Their immediate family would also be moved and reprogrammed, as well.

For the defective youth, the bonds of family were rebuilt in youth hostel.

Twinner reprogramming was only necessary for dual society parents. If surface parents moved immediately at their child's birth to the Thirdshift, the parental bond stayed intact and no reprogramming was necessary.

Few dual society parents existed. Birth defects were the exception with improved health care, and most opted to move with their child. Having the unique status of a Twinner also required designated Good Relations teams to move about with the parents during visitation, which was a burden to the leadership for such an archaic practice, but respect for all life was deemed the Goodness decree.

To the best of their ability, the Goodness Alliance of Nations chose where its people would thrive. A fulfilled life meant top production for all shifts, and by using science to test the emotional and physical needs of the people through profiles and audits, the evolution of the 24 hour society flourished as the population grew.

Thirdshift's underground society was a place for those who didn't meet the government surface standards. The Thirdshift world began as a damp, bleak and dirty confinement and developed to a pristine, solar-powered, state-of-the-art entertainment and medical complex in the deepest bowels of the channel. For *Twinner* visitations, these citizens weren't permitted in the subterranean caverns, but instead the tunnel entry, Block 86 processing, the medical wards and the cafeteria.

Tunnel culture developed after hundreds of years of rehabilitation. Thirdshift physicians developed better rebel reprogramming techniques and discovered that defectives could thrive through art-expression in painting, sculpting, writing, acting, singing, and individual oral storytelling.

Bea concluded that Crystal may want to find her way into the caverns, if she could convince the Peace Doctors to allow her to work on their theatrical costumes.

Bea had not experienced the underworld, but Sal had told her of its existence and she knew it had to be tremendous to impress Sal. She missed her husband dearly.

GLOBAL GOOD

Mark sat in Zahndra's cubical and played with the small flashing photo projector on her desk.

"Z, tell me about that photo." He clicked the button on its top to stop it.

Zahndra leaned over and clicked the small remote to let the photos continue to scroll. "Why?"

"Curious," he shrugged.

"That's my roommate, Sybille."

He picked up the eyeball shaped projector and flashed it on Zahndra's face. A photo of a bull's-eye appeared on her forehead. "I didn't know you like archery?"

A bowl of fruit, an apple, an orange and a banana flashed on her complexion.

She grabbed the projector, ignoring him. "Have you done digital paint?"

"No I haven't," Mark smiled wryly.

"Silly, it's the best new activity. The Entertainment Ministry opened up an old lab and charged up some vintage technology…"

"I know," he snipped, "and they flash an image on each of four walls and you get assigned a tablet to draw or paint the image while getting a mood scan."

"Isn't it great?"

Mark's smile pursed. "Ahh the mood scan… the colors reveal your temperament."

"Sure. It's so cool and I LOVE to paint!"

"The mood scan is accurate, you're aware." Mark looked to the ceiling and focused on a tile about four feet above them.

"Really?! Mine stayed blue. I love it, I just marvel at the colors of the room. Everyone has glowing wrists and the lights are dimmed, it's so intimate and they serve shaved ice in a rainbow of flavors, it's the best!"

Mark quickly bored of Zahndra's conversation and her clueless brain. He tossed the projector on the desk and it landed on its side, freezing on the image of Sybille inside their apartment. In the photo a gold glow washed out the right side of the picture, making Sybille appear fuzzy around her right elbow, hip and thigh. Zahndra loved the fusion of color and decided to keep the photo among her favorites.

"What's this really about?" Zahndra asked.

Mark looked up at the ceiling again, "Just doing my job."

Inside the control room of Global Good North's tower in the Arctic Circle, Eston Cote watched Mark pander to the camera. He wasn't certain what the younger man wanted to communicate, so he amped up the microchips in both Mark and Zahndra and heard the vague conversation about the photos. When Eston zoomed in on the photo he saw no threat and instead began scanning the sea of alternating images in other monitors from the North Region.

Eston rolled back in his chair and watched the sporadic images in different sections of the North. Each was programmed to flash in a red frame if a potential insurgency or hostile behavior was evident.

He depended on the Peace Doctors, Entertainment Ministry and the Monument Society to be his eyes and ears for the North, along with their counterparts in Good Relations.

A child of about eight years of age walked in with a tray of tea and placed it on Eston's credenza. "Please ask for the controllers to return to the booth," he motioned to the child.

Eston's annual visit was earlier than anticipated due to the urgent request of the Peace Doctors in the Arctic region. On September 14th some of the artifact container lids blew and at the same time a rumbling howl froze all monitoring for a period of twenty minutes. The staff couldn't communicate with GG and were blinded instantly by a brilliant light streaming out of one of the container hangars.

The Arctic was a city of container hangars that stored the world's finest works of art and artifacts that were counter-culture to Global Good. When the system was restored they urged Eston to come immediately. The period ten minutes prior to the occurrence jammed backup tapes, but through diligent effort they were able to get some grainy images.

The crew feared an earthquake or other natural disasters were causing the phenomenon. They bolted Hangar 40 with additional reinforcements but it didn't stop the huge stream of light that had softened but still streamed upward and through the roof of the facility. The noise subsided at the end of the first day, but the light continued.

When Eston flew in that morning on Global Good's transport plane, he had the pilot circle and fly over several times to see if Hanger 40 had suffered an explosion, but instead, was awed by the luminous light that seemed to pierce the building itself.

No one had been inside the storage facility since the incident, fearing exposure would consume them. Eston wasn't fearful as he knew the inventory and there were no warheads or explosives stored in the region. He felt certain that it was an atmospheric condition. But what concerned him more was that the light might cause the stored relics to deteriorate rapidly. He needed to get that under control.

Eston had the debonair, chiseled features of a more mature man. His temples were streaked salt and pepper on this day and, though graying wasn't permitted by Global Good to secure age equality, Eston didn't interact much outside of his regional partners and their staff and thus had the authority to make his own exceptions. The Quad met via satellite, so his Global colleagues only saw him on the quarterly summits.

His five foot eleven physique was lean like his peers, but his chest and biceps were fuller due to a weight training obsession that required more caloric intake. He took advantage of his status and added an additional meal to his daily procurement in order to keep metering green.

If he chose to see the citizens of the region, he usually did so during costume events when everyone had the chance to change their appearance for the day or evening. Then he could either wear his natural gray streaks or cover them as needed.

Eston's audits at age fourteen revealed an extraordinary photographic memory of history and data archival. The aging leaders watched his growth, grooming him for a top position at twenty five. He didn't have the investigative nature they sought, but to help him along they developed rigorous challenges around art history that engaged his curiosity and thus honed the detective within. They liked his inquisitive versus intrusive pursuit of knowledge. They weren't certain he was the appropriate direction for their next leader, but they needed his creative skills at data storage and his passion for preservation and history.

Eston, they knew, could easily maintain the museum pieces for another seventy years and develop a leader to follow. When Eston was installed as the leader of the GG North Quad he instigated the micro-chipping of all artifact containers and put them on the same mainframe as society. He wanted instant access to everything in the north and partitioned the files for his and his staff's access.

He also didn't want to travel much, but instead queue in the storage items and remote monitor, similar to the way GG did the region. Since all items were photographed and catalogued from inception of the GG initiative, Eston could peruse the items remotely and chronicle his knowledge and any research done on each object. It would take a lifetime, but he would enjoy registering his narrative to each piece.

Eston began with banned works of art that depicted violence and mutiny. He didn't engage so much with the content as with the talent that created such. He would spend hours describing the brush strokes that formed the images of embattlement and carefully describe the color and texture of the work.

His remote monitoring didn't record the incident of September 14th. It couldn't detect the compromised container. Instead his staff radioed him of the events.

The controllers walked into the booth and were hopeful for Eston's assessment.

"Men, Women," he stood, "I'm going to need you to open Hangar 40 and I'll need a few of your restoration crew to join me for some advisory discussions."

He continued, "It appears that the phenomenon is a supernatural occurrence."

One person raised their hand and Eston acknowledged the controller.

"We aren't familiar with the term 'supernatural occurrence'."

Eston was slightly annoyed, "But you ALL KNOW what is stored in Hangar 40."

SOBBING HEAP-OF-MAN

Mancy was a sobbing heap-of-man curled in a fetal position on the surgical waiting area floor. The performance art massacre was now a reality in his mind. Jewel was pacing the length of the room, angry at the sniveling excuse for a brother Mancy turned out to be.

"You…" he felt bile rising in his throat "…controlled… m-m-me!" He looked up at her, shaking violently and barely able to manage the convulsing shame that was causing him to heave.

"Troubled, are we?"

"W-w-what's th-the point, Jewel?" He was shivering from the emotional anguish.

"Honey," she squatted down, "we both know you had a choice. I can't make you do anything."

"Choice?"

She patted his hands. "Here, here, we've got work to do and the surgeons can fix Crystal. I need to get in my scrubs. Can you please pull it together? I've got to get Bea out of there before I go into the surgery unit."

"It's n-n-n-not j-j-just Crrrr-yssstal, it's th-the p-p-p-people I killed!" he curled up more tightly, "and th-the ones who w-w-w-were tr-tra-trampled to death."

Jewel folded her arms and just stared at him. His stuttering was annoying her.

"I n-n-never w-wanted…"

Jewel slapped the top of his head, hard.

His closed his eyes, flinching, and began to sob again, grabbing Jewel's ankles for support.

"You did Good." She placated him as if he were a well-behaved puppy.

"Good! G-g-good!" He looked up at her, "You don't know the meaning of Good?!"

"Means different things to different people," she mused nonchalantly.

"W-w-why c-c-c-couldn't you do th-the d-dirty w-w-w-work yourself?"

She stepped out of his grasp and sat on the floor beside him, stroking his hair and cradling him. "I guess it's time I tell you."

"W-w-w-what?"

"About our daddies… I mean growing up it didn't seem important, we were just kids and our daddies loved each other and they loved us. Clive knew I was different. I really didn't know I was different for a while." Jewel laughed softly.

"H-h-how?

"Stop talking honey, or I'll slap you again."

His watering eyes pleaded for answers.

"Clive's native country was rooted in spiritual warfare." She was now reflective and played with his hair, her demeanor loving.

It always confused him when she was hot and cold, but he didn't know her any other way. She was a chameleon to others, but in private she was manic or sullen, one or the other, most all of the time. Roberto and Clive had taught him to respect her uniqueness.

"S-sp-spiritual warfare?"

"Hasn't occurred in a long, long time."

"Spiritual?" he repeated, awaiting her definition.

"Don't even want to say the word, makes me gag."

Mancy sat up and took a few deep breaths and blew them out. They were both in their late twenties, but they would always be two little kids who liked to foot race. It seemed they were always competing.

"Mancy… I'm part human …" Jewel began.

"Part?"

"And part fallen angel," Jewel said without emotion. "Something happened recently that opened up this energy in me and it's like I'm finally free and in control. I read some writings that Clive stored in the attic where we used to play and it didn't make sense before …"

"Angel?" His sister's words fell between them without his comprehension, without explanation. "Recently?"

A FLY flew in through the air conditioner vent and buzzed around her head, landing on Mancy's shoulder.

Jewel leaned in and thunked it with her thumb and middle finger, "What a pest." She laughed hysterically.

One of the controllers asked Eston to open his remote processor. He stopped his meeting and flipped open the pocket size unit and saw the frozen image of Mancy and Jewel and the noted caption, **Insurrection Threat TS**. He played the video and realized what was happening.

He put his headset on and told the tower, "Guard Hangar 40!"

You Just Don't Understand

Blair materialized beside Sybille and motioned for her to keep quiet.

Zahndra had just returned home from work and Sybille heard her cohab knocking at the bedroom door. Blair nodded to let her in.

"Hey," Sybille acted interested.

"Everything ok?" Zahndra asked.

NO! Sybille wanted to say. She looked at Blair, who wasn't smiling, and replied, "Is there something wrong?"

"Ah, I'm fine," Zahndra brushed off Sybille's comment.

Sybille didn't respond.

"You like roasted rabbit, right? I'm going to the cafeteria soon. I heard it's pretty hearty."

Sybille was tempted. She was getting hungry but she looked at Blair for her answer. Blair was shaking her head no.

"I'm going to the supper club and then I'll catch some soccer at the arena." She knew Zahndra disliked sports.

"Okay, have fun," Zahndra turned to leave. Then she stopped and turned, staring at Sybille. "I had a visitor today…"

Sybille moved toward Blair and, though Zahndra couldn't see Blair, the two stood with their arms folded awaiting Zahndra's completed statement.

"Someone who was admiring the picture I took of you with the overexposed image at your side."

143

Sybille smiled at Blair.

Zahndra's mouth opened. "Why did you look over, like someone was there?"

"Just having fun with you," Sybille looked at Blair again and they were both amused. "You don't know me Z, Crystal and I have always been silly and you just don't understand."

Zahndra smiled reluctantly, "Why didn't you ask who the visitor was?"

"Ok, who was the visitor?" Sybille played along.

VITAL TO SOCIETY

Once Zahndra left Blair made a gagging sound. "Ewww, rabbit?"

Sybille looked surprised. "It's quite good. Have you tried it?"

"No! Where I come from, no one would brag about eating a rabbit or a rat." Blair made a face of utter distaste.

"What do you eat?" Sybille was fascinated.

"I used to eat fried chicken and barbecue pork sandwiches."

Sybille looked as sickened as Blair. "That's disgusting! The pigs at the zoo eat their own feces and chickens aren't much different from rats, they all scurry around on the ground. Besides, they stopped the practice of eating pigs, cows and large animals hundreds of years ago after the bacteria plague! The plague began in the pigs in the Far East. Our goats today provide milk, but otherwise, we don't eat impure meats.

Blair's mouth flew open, "In my day rats were impure."

"Rodents breed quickly and they don't carry disease because they're bred by Good!" Sybille was indignant.

"In my time we used to say you are what you eat." Blair grinned.

"Then I'm proud. Rodents are a staple. It means I'm a vital part of society."

"Well, that is true Sybille, that's the reason I'm here. You are vital to society."

"And why do you say *in my time*?" Sybille asked.

"I'm an intercessor, Sybille. I'm not physically here," Blair said quietly.

Sybille paused, "Like Frank."

Blair began to de-crystallize.

"Don't!" Sybille demanded.

Blair stopped and reformed her full self. "I need you to take what I'm about to say seriously."

Sybille was glad Blair didn't leave again.

"If you get in any serious trouble I want you to shout, **Michael!** at the top of your voice and then ask for whatever you need and it should be provided." Blair was firm.

"The winged man?" Sybille ventured a guess.

"Yes, this is very serious, Sybille." Blair was stern.

"Then why can't I just ask for Michael to return Bea, Frank and Crystal now?"

"Are you in serious trouble right now?"

"Why can't I ask?" Sybille wondered.

"You have work to do first."

"But you're saying I'm going to get into some bad situation and need to ask for help?"

"You might... okay, you will."

Sybille's eyes got big.

Blair shrugged her shoulders. "Sorry, I'm just telling you what I know."

"So I don't have a choice?"

Blair paused. "Well... I guess you do."

"So I want to ask for them to return now!" Sybille was impatient.

"What if that doesn't work?" Blair asked Sybille.

"Then I'll do it your way." Sybille conceded.

Blair laughed. "Ok."

"Michael!"

Then Sybille heard Zahndra running toward her room, followed by a rapid knocking on her door. A FLY flew in behind Zahndra. "Did you call out? I thought I heard you say, Michael?"

Blair de-crystallized, shaking her head.

FORBIDDEN IN THE
CURRENT AGE

A female controller stepped forward, "We know religious artifacts are stored in Hangar 40, but of what significance are they?"

Eston realized there was no way these people knew what the potential threat might be. "What do you understand about the artifacts?"

"Only that they belonged to prior civilizations and are forbidden in the current age, but I'm not sure why."

"Humph." Eston pondered what to say next and what to withhold.

"Should we know more?"

"Let's say, you might be getting an education very soon."

The controllers, a dozen in all, just looked at each other and didn't speak. Their directive was to follow Eston's instructions and when necessary seek advisement, but otherwise, they were to go about their jobs monitoring, guarding and living life.

"Sir," a gentleman stepped forward.

"Yes?" Eston responded.

"We've suspended our entertainment privileges as we weren't certain if an evacuation was in order."

Eston was surprised by their alarm. "I understand this recent occurrence has you all concerned, but your lives should not be disrupted further. The beam streaming into the sky is not harmful, on the contrary, you might become energized by its properties, but please, do not open Hangar 40 unless I am in attendance."

"So you don't want to inspect it? What is our instruction then regarding Hangar 40?" They wanted firm answers.

Eston realized his elders had not encountered any major trouble in hundreds of years, but now in his tenth year of leadership he had the challenge of a lifetime. "I'm aware of its contents and you are at the safest place on earth."

Their eyes grew big and Eston knew he had said more than necessary, but he wanted calm to be restored.

A hand was raised.

"Yes."

"Is there a place that we need to be watchful for in our monitoring of the North?" One team member asked.

"No more than usual." Eston assured them.

A sigh of relief seemed to fall over the room and Eston started to adjourn the meeting, but changed his mind. "Could you ask the little girl who brought me tea to come in? I have a few questions for her."

The staff all looked confused.

"But sir, there are no children here?" Another spoke up.

DEMON THRUST

Blair's journal

Someday somebody's gonna read this and think I'm crazy.

I just don't know how to say this any clearer, I saw demons today! Hundreds of them swarming like gnats and they were not small - they were the size of a medium cat and gross! Gray flesh with big heads and saw blade teeth, kind of like monkeys but more like naked babies, and they were attacking Sister Jo. One actually possessed her for a few minutes and Michael pulled it out of her. I saw that!

God sent me to the church to keep Father Murphy from exiting. (Remember when I journaled that God wanted me to get Father's attention somehow? Well...) Thank goodness Michael was there to save Sister Jo. I just don't understand how God decides who will get archangel protection and who fends for themself?

I also overheard my parents arguing recently about who I am more like, are they jealous? Believe me, they wouldn't have wanted to be me today! My mother would have had a heart attack and my father would have been stupid enough to think he could help Michael fight! The fact that I see St. Michael the Archangel is crazy enough, but to witness Satan's helpers!

I don't know how I am going to grow up normal. Who will I ever be able to talk to other than Sister Jo? Father Murphy doesn't know how to handle anything supernatural, in fact, he's blind to it!

I just don't know why God would show a dumb kid all of this and his devoted priest can't see a thing? Of course, I already know the answer. He's not ready. Like I am? What makes me ready? I didn't ask for this, but neither did Moses or Noah. It's all about saving people.

Peace, Blair

CLIVE'S SEED

Insurrection **Threat TS** continued flashing on Eston's keycard and he knew it was only a matter of time before the surface citizens would discover their brethren below.

His briefing was interrupted with the news of the Mancy Black Mutiny and massacre footage. He asked that the movement of citizens and bodies to TSA be completed and reprogramming commence immediately.

"Let's get suited up, we're going into Hangar 40." Eston motioned to two control room personnel, a man and woman.

The answers he needed were there after all, he couldn't delay any further. He reviewed and interviewed his staff repeatedly and no breach of protocol or insurrection threat was evident prior to the September 14th system jam. The little girl who served him tea was never seen by his staff, yet she was very real to him.

The three geared up in parkas, gloves, climate designed coveralls, boots and face masks that kept the moisture from their breath regulated with the cold dry air outside. Each had a headset that allowed them to talk among themselves without exposing their faces to the cold.

"Once inside," Eston said, "we'll determine the threat procedures and see if there is any way this corresponds to the uprising in a lower Manhattan supper club…"

The female controller interrupted, "I wonder how an insurrection that far away will affect us?"

"You'd be surprised," he answered.

Crystal awoke in the recovery room. Her eyes tried to focus on the white ceiling that suddenly turned into the image of Jewel's beautiful but unsettling face.

Jewel stood over Crystal and was quite pleased, "Looks like you'll be up to the next challenge soon."

Crystal shook her head, no. She was now fortified with a supplement to accelerate the healing process. It not only restored her fragile ankle bones but it also energized her mind and she was no longer fearful of Jewel.

"I believe you're right," Crystal raised herself up to her elbows. "You may have put me in this situation, but you aren't holding me here." She hadn't felt this bold or outspoken since she was fourteen. The energy was electric and she wanted to jump off the hospital bed and get in Jewel's face.

Jewel gave her a maniacal smile, "Got our confidence back, did we?" She took a step back and sneered at the younger woman.

"Yes, **I** did and this isn't a **we**," Crystal pointed at Jewel, then to herself. "I'm not helping you."

Jewel began to cackle. "Of course you are," she moved to the foot of the bed and held tightly to both of Crystal's wrapped ankles. "You are here for no other reason."

Crystal felt a surge of adrenaline and at almost lightning speed she sat up in an Indian squat out of Jewel's reach. She had no pain. Her vision was like a laser beam now. She stared at Jewel. "I had a dream in surgery. I watched them work on my ankles and I floated around throughout this place and the people look so different and the things they do... I also saw you with Mancy and he was crying. There was a muddy red glow that hugged your body and it turned black at times. You weren't nice and when I returned to my physical body, my mind kept saying that my walk was not about physical ability, but the journey."

Jewel knew it was time. Just as planned, she had stirred Crystal's soul, but she would need reinforcements if she was going to trap Michael.

Eston removed his face gear and nodded to the two crew members accompanying him to do the same. They were now inside the expansive shelter and the light that poured upward was softening. A crate top was fragmented in confetti jagged toothpick-sized chips spanning the immediate six foot radius of the open container. Not a solid piece existed.

Eston grabbed a tall utility ladder, determined to look inside the box and see what damage had been done to the contents. Opening his microprocessor, he keyed in the catalogue number burned into the outside of the wooden carton: V13. He ascended the ladder rungs when he heard the swoosh noise that indicated his search results were ready. He tried to ignore it as he made his way up, but his curiosity got the best of him. He dug into his pocket and grabbed the processor, flipping it open.

The female crew member called up to him, pointing to the debris. "Should we bag the fragments for the lab?"

Eston ignored her as he muttered, "Remains…"

The woman waited.

The screen read: VATICAN Remains. He shut the processor off. "Send word to standby," he looked down at them.

The male crew member radioed the control center.

Eston reached a level where he could peer inside and saw 2 metal boxes. One appeared as though something had escaped through a large gaping hole. It looked pried open by way of an industrial can opener. Metal shards protruded out from the carton and the other box was still sealed. The one that was blown open read: `Relic of St. Paul`.

"Really," Eston spoke to himself. He seemed to understand its significance. "Please handle the remains with care," he spoke into the box.

What would make the carton of an ancient saint's remains explode, he wondered?

The two crew members used biohazard vacuums to capture the smallest fragments surrounding the crate for quarantine and testing.

Eston remained at the top looking down into the container.

Crystal got to her feet when Jewel left the room and gave her legs a try.

She was under the influence of a super vitamin compound and amazed how strong she felt. Careful to avoid breaking her ankles again, she gingerly stepped out of the hospital room in her soft cast boots to look for Bea.

Crystal rounded the corner and ran into Mancy, who had the bloodshot look of a wild beast. He glared down at her, but didn't seem to recognize her. She stepped back against the wall and gave him the space to keep going in the direction of Block 86.

She decided to follow behind him about ten paces when unexpectedly the pain became more intense below her calves. Her legs might carry her if she could tolerate the burning.

As Mancy rounded the corner to the group cell, Crystal spied Bea talking with some younger detainees. One of them pointed at Mancy and then Crystal made eye contact with the older woman.

Bea watched, but didn't react to the wild man who was now making growling noises as he got closer. He shouted at the crowd. "There is one among you who will deliver the enemy to me!"

Crystal felt a force pushing her closer to Mancy.

"I think you have it all wrong," she challenged.

He turned, now hunched over, and snarled, "YOU!" He pounced toward her.

Crystal froze.

Mancy bounced off of an invisible force between him and Crystal. He growled louder and the detainees began screaming.

Crystal closed her eyes, expecting the worst. She could feel his heat in front of her and very slowly peeked her lids open to see the hazy vapor holding Mancy back.

A voice came from in front of her saying to Mancy, "Eject … eject the beast!"

Mancy's eyes bugged out in a ferocious rage. He began shaking violently, throwing himself at the vapor wall and barking furiously.

Crystal closed her eyes and stood still. If the energy field dissipated it would be the end of her.

Was this her fate? To be betrayed, maimed, relocated, operated on and now she'd be torn to shreds by a fanatical monster?

Her adrenaline rush was gone and she felt numb.

Without warning Mancy collapsed to the floor. The crowd in Block 86 applauded as though she had given a command performance and at the same time, she felt the most intense fire in her ankles that caught her breath.

"Walk here, Crystal," Bea shouted and Crystal followed the sound of the reassuring voice.

"Sit here," Bea pointed to the floor outside the cell and Crystal slid down the bars and began to cry. "He's going to tear me to shreds when he wakes up." She was now exhausted.

Bea moved to a position just behind Crystal and spoke softly. "He won't know. Do you understand?"

Crystal was inconsolable as Mancy began to stir. Crystal drew her knees to her chest and massaged her ankles. She placed her face into her knees and mumbled that she wanted Sybille.

A sound of wheels approached from a distance. Everyone remained quiet.

Two orderlies rolled a gleaming metal gurney into view, plucked Mancy off the floor and strapped him onto the stretcher, then rolled him away. Even Bea was astonished that they didn't seem to know Crystal was in the room.

Crystal sobbed. "I miss Sybille. I want to go our apartment."

Those inside the cell were muttering similar sentiments.

Bea stroked the top of her head, "We will ALL be fine."

She addressed the group loudly. "Button it up everyone. We need to be strong."

Eston zoomed in on the monitor and replayed the scene. He couldn't understand how the small blonde in the white hospital sheath was holding the wild man from harming her. The tall man seemed to be pushing himself against her, yet she had some control over him and he wasn't able to negotiate around her. Eston keyed in the ID screen and saw Crystal Lundgren and Mansford Black a.k.a. Mancy Black. They were surface residents who had been moved to TSA for holding. He keyed in the incident report and watched the surveillance video of Mancy's performance again and did a 360 degree search of the audience, spotting Crystal with Jewel and a few other table mates. It seemed the two women were enjoying an exchange and then moments later the redhead stood and sounded an alarm.

Then he replayed the footage of Mancy and Crystal at TSA again and still couldn't figure out how Crystal held Mancy back. Given that the club incident went dark after the initial ax swing at the Entertainment Minister, he could only assume that Crystal had put Jewel and Mancy up to this.

Eston held his control switch over Jewel and read her bio. She was the surrogate sister of Mansford Black and a practicing nurse for the Health Counsel. He scrolled down and read further.

Her father Clive was the son of Porter Tallon, a guard in the Monument Society of Region 3. Porter worked the Clock Tower Waterway and Clive's mother, Quinn Taylor Tallon, had been a teacher. It was believed that Porter placed Clive on a petroleum ship when he and Quinn developed the bacteria infection that swept their region. Their son was still healthy when they gave him to the ship's captain, Ives Black.

The infant Clive was adopted by the Black Miner family who ran the transport fleet for The Goodness Alliance. Raised with Ives son, Roberto Black, the boys fell in love as children and later partnered. They each wanted a child that would represent the family Clive had lost and the loving people who took Clive in.

Eston couldn't open the report on Quinn. He swiped his secured access that required a further code and he keyed in the word Denied.

Goodness leaders chose to code historic information on families whose prestige, wealth, privilege, shocking or horrific lineage could deny them equal standing in society. Protecting their heritage meant that only in cases where they were under suspicion would the Quad unlock their report, review and possibly put offspring and other family members under intense FLY watch.

A few clicks later and he had what he needed.

Clive's seed had brought about Jewel. Jewel was her Grandmother Quinn's granddaughter! It seemed the gene had skipped a generation as Clive didn't appear to have his daughter's challenges.

Now he knew, both Jewel and Crystal were threats!

Bea whispered in Crystal's ear, "It's time."

Crystal raised her head, her hair covered her face and she turned to Bea. "I don't understand?"

"Jewel is coming back for you. You have something she wants, what is it?"

"I don't know."

"It's your connection with Sybille. She is the only thing that connects all of us." Bea clued her in.

"But I don't know how to get to Sybille." Crystal protested.

"Jewel does."

Eston reviewed the tapes again and again and tried to connect Crystal to Jewel and Mancy. Researching Crystal's background, he found Sybille Malone to be her cohab from youth hostel, and as he trolled the archives and found the damaged tape from 9.14.

He saw Sybille open the tenth floor window and then the tape went to snowy distortion. He keyed in some commands to repair the tape and saw grainy footage that continued until another woman walked up to her.

Eston looked for FLY footage from her building and watched Sybille standing on the ledge and saw her climb back in. Then the tape stopped and went to fuzz. How was this not flagged for a threat? He replayed it over and over and then looked at the date stamp again.

It happened at the same exact time the container lid blew in Hangar 40!

MEET JOAN

Sybille did her best to just keep working and looking for her friends. It was tough, but she had to act as though everything was normal.

And Blair hadn't come back as promised, so now it was a waiting game.

Sybille was presenting a new material idea to Fabric Council members when Blair suddenly materialized in front of her.

Alongside Blair was another woman. Blair stated matter-of-factly, "We're going to need Joan."

Sybille was in mid-sentence when Blair had begun talking. She had just proposed a new protective material that was lightweight but gave the body protection from snow and rain. With this new material the winter overcoat would provide warmth, comfort and could even be stored in residents' apartments.

It was Sybille's intent to work with the council to slowly eliminate spring storage, using that budget to add additional garments to the daily wardrobe. She had to begin somewhere, since approvals could take years. She also wanted to add a blue colorblock to the back of the jacket. The same blue she saw in Blair's shirt the day they met.

"Joan," Sybille realized she had spoken out loud.

Zahndra blinked, "Did you just name the material Joan?"

Sybille didn't reply. She just looked at the group seated at the long oval table and then back at the two glowing women in front of her.

Zahndra looked around the table and back to Sybille. "You said the fabric would be protective and … *Joan*…" Her cohab was being understanding and helpful, but was equally confused.

Sybille looked at Blair and Joan, who were nodding in agreement.

"Joan is my project name," Sybille said reluctantly.

"We don't understand," several table members were looking at one another.

Sybille stared at the two women sandwiched in a barrier of beaded light between her and the council members, finding her words as she spoke them. "I'd like to propose we wear..."

"Armor," Joan spoke.

"Armor," Sybille echoed.

Someone spoke up, "Armor, or Joan?"

"My fabric proposal is Joan… and the jacket is Armor," Sybille was beginning to like the idea. "Our theatrical plays have knights in armor who sweep maidens off their feet… and we all deserve a suit of armor to protect us… from the elements that could harm us."

Zahndra spoke up, "I like the armor, but I'm not getting the Joan?"

Someone else echoed Zahndra's sentiment, "Why Joan?"

"We have fabrics with blends of cotton, wool, etc. Those fabrics could have a new description…" Sybille offered.

Blair shook her head for Sybille to stop talking, "Just ask them to vote so we can move on."

Before Sybille could suggest anything the group began to assess the idea.

Sybille excused herself and headed to the restroom.

"Way to go, Syb…" Blair joked once they were in the restroom. The glowing woman laughed as Sybille sat on the counter top.

"How about you not come to my work, or at least give me some warning?" Sybille longed for understanding of Blair's comings and goings, "And you didn't come back like you said you would."

Joan stood at attention beside Blair, awaiting her turn to speak.

"Ok, but we don't have much time," Blair said. "This is Joan, she's a saint, and she knows a lot about fighting, so she's going to help you."

Sybille's eyes got big and her mouth flew open. "Fighting? Wait, is this Sister Jo?"

"No. And yes, fighting. Sister Jo is a saint, but she's not joining us." Blair said. "I'm not really sure if you'll need Joan, but she's available, so I figured between Michael and Joan, you'll be covered."

"I'll be covered?" Sybille was more confused.

"Stop repeating after me."

Sybille turned to Joan, "It's nice to meet you. I'm not sure what Blair is talking about."

Joan was dressed in archaic French battle armor, her hair cropped short in pageboy style. When she faced Sybille her features were plainly elegant and glowing. "Blair wants me to help you fight your enemy, and Michael will also be with us. Blair doesn't want to fight."

"I don't want to fight!" Sybille said. "How about you and Michael fight and I stay with Blair?"

"It's your battle," Joan said. "If you don't fight, a lot of people could be sacrificed unnecessarily."

Sybille couldn't believe what she was hearing.

"Calm down." Blair stressed, "I had to go through a lot to be here for you. You've read my diary. We're chosen. You can refuse, it's your free will, but if you do, you have to know that whatever happens, you made the choice."

Sybille grew quiet. She had no clue how to fight—or what fighting really was. She just knew that it was not done without consequence.

"Besides," Blair reasoned, "I'm not technically a saint, yet. I have to have several miracles attributed to me before I'm considered…"

"Miracles?" Sybille was very confused.

"It's kind of a long story, but to keep it simple, saints are people who were/are devoted to God, many were martyred…"

"Martyred?" Sybille was again perplexed.

"Just follow along before someone comes into the restroom."

Sybille nodded.

"Anyway, I've earned one stripe with you not jumping off the ledge. The diary got you interested in living and now I have to help you to the next stage, that's why I brought Joan."

Joan interjected, "My battle was big, too."

Blair nodded her head in agreement and pointed at Joan, "That's why I got her!"

REPROGRAMMING TONIGHT

Jewel met the stretcher in the infirmary and gave Mancy an injection. He woke almost immediately, feeling tired.

"Snap out of it," Jewel slapped his face. Just then a Peace Doctor walked in and asked Jewel if her patient needed a doctor.

"He's fine," she smiled prettily.

"We need you, then." The doctor informed her. "We're reprogramming tonight and it's going to be labor intensive with the number …"

Mancy looked over at Jewel with wide eyes.

She gave him a stern look to keep him shut up.

"We want to begin with the patient Crystal."

Jewel had to think quick, "Beatrice would be the one to start with."

The Peace Doctor looked at his charts, "She is a Sage Monument Guard. No, we'll need her to bring the residents to triage, they trust her."

LIMITED ACCESS

Mark followed Baker into the tunnel. Their contrasting uniforms were met with confused stares by the prisoners of Block 86, who wore Dayshift light gray garb. Mark was in the darker charcoal and very obviously belonged to the Nightshift.

Baker stood before the detainees as Mark stood aside, his arms folded behind his back.

"The unfortunate circumstances that brought you here were not of your design, we understand," Baker addressed them in a clear, confident tone. "However, to make you more comfortable in your new surroundings, we are going to bring your families in to join you."

Many smiled and sighed in relief.

Bea sat on the bench, stoically, her arms folded across her chest while she listened. She knew the reprogramming speech.

Baker scanned the cell looking for Crystal. Eston Cote had asked her to personally handle the girl's charge. She wasn't really certain of Crystal's involvement. Good Relations had limited access to Quad reporting and since the girl was like family, she hoped she would receive cooperation.

"We are missing someone?" Baker asked.

Bea stood. "Crystal Lundgren is in the infirmary, healing from injuries."

Baker looked hard at Bea, she knew the woman and respected her work.

Mark chimed in, "To the infirmary."

A blind TSA orderly spoke up, "I'll take you, sir."

Mark gawked at the tall pale man. His eye sockets were sunken in and his head was shaven clean, his white uniform starched and crisp. He had an instrument attached to his wrist that gave him guidance. Mark walked around him several times just staring.

"Please do," Mark said.

Baker nodded to Bea and then departed down the sanitary white hall to Crystal's room.

Crystal was strapped down again with her arms and legs tied to the underframe of the bed. She was also tied at the forehead and had a cloth jammed in her mouth.

Baker was shocked. What could the girl have done to deserve this horrid treatment?

Mark didn't notice Baker's reaction, but was curious about Crystal. He got on his knees, observing the knots under the bed, and how her body was arranged on it.

Crystal's eyes got bigger as she tried to speak to Sybille's mother in choked muffled noises. She was equally confused about why Mark was with Baker.

Baker asked the orderly to remove her gag. Then she realized the man couldn't see her.

"I'll do it." Baker leaned over and removed the gag herself.

"I'm so glad you're here Mother Malone," Crystal gasped.

Mark stopped and stared at Crystal. "Why do you call her Mother?"

"Are you here for Sybille?" Crystal asked Mark.

Baker looked puzzled this time. "Why do you ask him that?"

"Can you please untie me? This is painful." Crystal begged.

Baker asked Mark to do so.

Two Peace Doctors entered the room, followed by Jewel and Mancy, who was now dressed as an orderly.

Baker addressed them, "I need to speak with Crystal as part of a Good Relations assignment. You may begin processing Block 86."

Jewel smiled sweetly at Baker, "I'm Crystal's nurse, let me help."

Baker looked through her cool confidence and asked, "Is this your handiwork?"

Jewel nodded.

Mark struggled with the knots. Crystal kept her mouth shut, except to moan when he tugged at the straps.

"Why is an artist in an orderly uniform?" Baker commented. "He should be in the Block."

No one answered.

Mark stopped and addressed the room, "We are here to make certain reprogramming commences and completes. We need to speak with her," he pointed to Crystal. "...and we need refreshments."

Baker rolled her eyes. How could he think about food there was no procurement?

"The rest of you can begin the greater job at hand and give us some space," Mark concluded.

Jewel was delighted, "I'll get some tea and cakes."

She left, along with the Peace Doctor, the blind orderly and Mancy.

"You've got to get me out," Crystal urged. "What is reprogramming?"

Mark closed the door. "What did you do?"

Baker shook her head, "We know what happened, but how?"

"This is very strange," Crystal said, "really strange..."

"Get ON with it," Mark said.

"Sybille had a crush on you," Crystal told Mark. "She was sad because she knew you'd never be able to date..."

"My Sybille was considering a Nightshift partner?" Baker seemed insulted.

"Yes, so she began distancing herself from me and I tried to help... I wanted her to sort it out and keep from setting off meters. She wasn't emotionally well."

Baker was somber.

Crystal continued, "She knew it was wrong. I couldn't help her. Our friendship was strained. I started doing things on my own. That's how I ended up in the club with Jewel watching Mancy and the Jax Band."

Mark sat on the bed beside her, "Did you know what Jewel was going to do that night?"

"How come you aren't even asking about Sybille?" Crystal became indignant. "Does her crush on you not mean *anything*?"

"No," Mark answered candidly.

"But you teased her," Crystal was mad. "I saw you flirting on the train!"

"I'll admit, I was, but it's not what you think."

Baker wasn't certain what was going on between these young people. "Get on with the story before Jewel gets back," Baker insisted.

"I didn't even know Jewel, I just sat at her table and she acted like she knew I would."

Baker shook her head. "How would she know?"

"It was fate," Jewel said as she rolled in a tea cart.

The woman's voice sent shivers through Crystal's body.

"Have some tea," Jewel stopped the cart and poured.

"How about you tell us what took place," Baker crossed her arms and leaned against the wall.

"You may as well know," the redhead laughed. "The time has come."

WHERE YOU FIT IN

Blair's journal

OK, I have to tell you about St. Paul and Michael. Michael is the protector angel and St. Paul was very important to the continuation of Christianity.

So this is where <u>you</u> fit in, Sybille.

If there weren't a Sybille, there wouldn't be a continuation of God in THIS world. You don't know him yet, just like Paul didn't really know Jesus until he was blinded on the Damascus road. You both are important to leading the faithful.

Don't get all freaked out trying to understand. Everything will make sense.

Peace,

Blair

SOMEONE ELSE'S SKIN

Zahndra walked into the restroom and saw the golden glow on either side of Sybille.

"What's going on?"

Sybille's eyes were shimmering in tears. She didn't speak.

"I'm going with you," Zahndra said.

Sybille didn't discourage her. Blair and Joan nodded that they needed the cohab. Blair said to Sybille, "Tell her we need to go below."

Zahndra had never been in direct communication with the Quad since her support training and initial assignment. As Eston's protégé's it was Zahndra's job to assist Sybille, report back, and not lose sight of the woman. Global Good would monitor their activities and have backup security waiting, should they have any problems.

Sybille now felt as though she were seeing through someone else's eyes, living in someone else's skin. It reminded her of some of Blair's writing and she knew that whatever happened, she wouldn't feel pain, because it wasn't her physical being that was in control. It was the *Spirit*.

Zahndra brought Sybille to the Global Good Family Center.

"I'm changing your keycard to Twinner status and then I'll take you. Stay here."

Sybille didn't say a word, she just sat stoic, obeying orders. Joan and Blair stayed on either side of her.

Jewel was called into a consult by a Peace Doctor before she revealed her identity, which gave Baker a chance to regroup.

Baker overheard TSB receiving a signal that a Twinner was arriving, assisted by Zahndra Iyer, and she wondered why her daughter's other cohab was coming to the tunnel. "Mark, could you meet Zahndra while I speak with Crystal?"

"Zahn... what is she...?"

"Escorting a Twinner, I'm not sure why, but please check it out."

Baker moved closer to Crystal, "what does Jewel want with you?"

"I really don't know," Crystal insisted.

"Are you familiar with reprogramming?" Crystal shook her head no.

"They erase your memories, you become a new person." Baker's emotions were now getting the best of her. She had always been able to separate herself from the job and now she was weakening. "I can't move you. I'm sorry..." Baker wanted to hug the girl, but knew it would make it harder for both of them.

Crystal nodded understanding as she choked on a sob, "The only thing I... know," Crystal tried to be brave, "Well I don't really know, I was moving around in a dream state during the surgery..." Crystal was now tearing up. "I ...I heard Jewel tell Mancy she was a fallen angel."

"Mark?"

Sybille was confused by his presence here, yet hopeful that they were together by design.

He was equally surprised. "You're not a Twinner…"

Zahndra looked at the two of them and remembered his earlier inquiry about the photo she'd taken… Seeing them together was unsettling. She interrupted their thoughts, "I need to get Sybille to Crystal, please."

Sybille's eyes welled up. She needed to see her friend.

Eston's aircraft returned to Manhattan early. On the flight in he dampened his hair and carefully covered his graying temples with some dark theatrical greasepaint. He would be entering the shifts and wanted to blend in. He needed to give both the Entertainment Ministry and Monument Society a directive for the new challenges that would ensue.

Taking no chances he reserved the 3rd floor of Sky Tower for this meeting. They would soon be broadcasting to The Quad and assigned personnel.

Frank and Paul stood in the back and watched as Eston entered the room. Frank turned to Paul, "Sybille pulling the diary released you?"

Paul nodded, "And it set off other forces at the same time, Francis."

Frank's voice was a whisper, "Where is this Blair you keep talking about?"

"Shh," Paul silenced him.

The cameras were being positioned and microphones tested.

Eston stepped away from the podium for a moment to shake hands with some of the people immediately in front of him.

Then the signal came and he moved back into position to speak, "Good day and evening to my fellow Quad members and Global Good. I am here to address a threat of a potential global holocaust."

This was met by a communal gasp.

He looked around the room for faces to connect with, as well as scanning for possible insurgents. "The only way I know to truly present this is to give you some Goodness history, as I am the archivist. Our society… in the most elementary description," he refused to read from notes—he wanted them to understand on a very personal level, "has been built on community, trust, reliance on our brethren to help keep the mechanisms of the world running efficiently, and most importantly seeking the Good within each one of us."

The crowd murmured approval.

"However, in so doing we abolished world religions in favor of one belief, Goodness. Good was the one element all faiths had in common. Each religion felt their belief was good, that their religion was the way society should live and in the repopulation of the world after the bacteria plague, the statesmen of the remaining world governments formed Global Good."

Mark, Baker, Sybille and Crystal huddled over Baker's keycard screen to watch Eston explain the coming threat, but were interrupted by Jewel.

"Time's up kiddies…" She was no longer in her nurse uniform, but draped in a blood red gown that accentuated her figure. Jewel appeared to have something hidden behind her back. Mancy wore black attire from head to toe and seemed sedate.

"I'll tell you all you need to know." She grabbed at Baker's hand. "Give me that," Jewel took the processor and tossed it to the floor.

A scream came from the hallway and Jewel knew the voice to be Bea's.

"Finally!" Jewel was thrilled that Bea was beginning reprogramming. "Where was I?"

Sybille stepped forward. "You were going to explain God to us."

Jewel spat at the girl. "You woke the devil in me, now!" She grabbed for Sybille.

Blair and Joan materialized and shook their heads no to Sybille, this wasn't the time. They departed to seek reinforcements. "We'll be back," Blair promised.

Jewel's maniacal laugh then filled the room. "I read the letters my grandmother left for my father." She shook the letter she had hidden from them. "And I've also read from a book Mancy's grandfather left him."

She delighted in her own revelations. "It seems we were all destined to be here, but instead of Michael helping you perpetuate the 'faith', I'm going to kill him!"

"Who is Michael?" Baker asked Sybille.

"The winged man in my dreams," Sybille whispered.

Baker's mouth fell open.

"My grandmother Quinn was a guardian angel who fell in love with the man she protected, Porter Tallon." She waved the letter in front of them. "It was through his own human stupidity that he was injured, though she tried to shield him. She asked for…" Jewel gagged, "… for her fellow guardians to pray for his recovery."

Baker glanced from Jewel to her daughter, who seemed to understand the wild woman's story.

"Guardians have only one human to defend in their lifetime and once that assignment is finished, they become a member of the choir of angels. Grandmother asked to step down." Jewel seemed proud then tore up the letter.

She turned to Sybille, "It would have been so much easier had you come to the supper club instead of Crystal. I waited every night…" Jewel pointed at Sybille. In a flick her wrist she threw the young woman across the room.

Sybille's eyes widened in shock as on impact she hit the wall, cracked the plaster and was knocked unconscious.

Baker lunged at Jewel. The demon redhead threw Baker atop Sybille and turned to Crystal and Mark, who were huddled together. "You irritate me!" She grabbed each of them up with her fists and howled in their faces.

She dropped Mark to the floor and proceeded to choke Crystal, "You delivered Sybille as planned, but I have no further need for you."

Sybille came to and saw Crystal, her throat clutched in Jewel's hands, and she screamed, "**Michael!**"

A roar burst through the sound barrier and the enormous winged man was there, pulling Jewel off of Crystal.

Eston fell to the floor in the rumbling earthquake that sent furnishing, fixtures and bodies bouncing off of one another.

Paul and Frank nodded to each other and rose up to hover over the group.

"Have no fear," Frank addressed the people in the room.

Eston could barely get to his feet when he was overcome at this sight and fell to his knees in reverence. "Who are you?"

"I am Paul and this is Francis," Paul addressed Eston.

"St. Paul," Eston realized.

"We need you to open the lines of communication and be ready to speak to *all* people."

Jewel got to her feet and looked at Mancy with annoyance. Without warning she flicked her wrist and tossed him against the wall next to Sybille and Baker. "You'll just get in my way!"

Michael grabbed Jewel by both shoulders, his eyes burning into hers. "To think you were one of us."

"I'm only half human, like your messiah was half human," she attempted to lick Michael's face. "We're meant for each other."

Michael let her go. "Do not blaspheme the Lord."

"*Your* Lord. Not mine." Jewel smiled.

"What are you planning?" He commanded.

"Just to have little fun with you, Michael."

"Quinn should never have stepped down." Michael's voice boomed.

Jewel sneered, "It seems your God gave my grandmother an option."

"Guardians are not supposed to fall in love with the humans they protect." Michael affirmed.

"It takes two to tango, Michael." Jewel's cackle bounced off the walls.

"Porter fell in love with a woman. He never knew her as his guardian. Quinn knew better than to engage with mortals. She knew that having a child opened the chance for her offspring to develop demon blood."

"Demon blood." Jewel laughed. "Sounds exciting."

"Quinn became a good woman …. and mother." Michael defended Quinn's memory.

"And humans and angels are susceptible to temptation, ain't it a shame." Jewel sing-songed and skipped around Michael.

"Being human doesn't become you, Jewel."

"Actually it does," she gave him an evil grin.

"Quinn's love for Porter produced a loving man, your father Clive. Clive was at risk, but had no understanding of his ancestry pool."

Jewel marveled at Michael's control. "Funny, Daddy had her letters. After all, I found them in his belongings." Jewel blew Michael a kiss.

"It's regretful." Michael said. "Human's have a way of ignoring their family history and the treasures of their ancestors."

"My great, great grandfather's book…" Mancy mumbled from his slumped position.

Jewel laughed. Her eyes darted around the room. She seemed pleased by the events that brought them together.

Blair re-materialized. "Ask Mancy about the book," she nudged a waking Sybille.

"About the book?" Sybille managed.

Mancy was sad as he spoke to Sybille. "Jewel destroyed the book."

Sybille was still foggy from the fall.

Jewel screamed for Mancy to shut up. "Dear brother!"

"You shouldn't have burned it." Mancy moaned.

"It was the memory of that picture book that gave me the idea to find Sybille. I was always restless, but it wasn't until a recent tremor stimulated my awareness… I knew…"

Those conscious murmured in astonishment.

Sybille was shocked.

Jewel turned to Michael. "Mancy and I read it over and over as kids. I marveled at how the story centered on a teenager who writes a diary for a girl named Sybille."

Jewel then stared at Blair.

Blair de-crystallized in fear. Only Sister Jo, her parents and Mo knew about the diaries.

"No," Mancy stood and addressed his sister. "I'm t-tired of being your p-puppet."

Mancy walked up to Michael, "Jewel became obsessed by the picture book. We found it in an old trunk our fathers kept in the attic."

Jewel added, "That's also where Quinn's letters were." She winked at Michael.

Blair materialized next to Mancy, "You're Mo's Grandson?" The small woman realized.

Mancy looked at Blair, puzzled.

Sybille realized, "He can see you!"

Mancy stepped back, "I don't know you."

"Mo wanted to meet Michael, it all makes sense," Blair said.

Mo materialized through Mancy's body and Mancy shivered.

"Hi Michael," Mo was thrilled and looked at everyone else. Mark, Baker and Crystal couldn't see him.

Jewel screamed. "I'm getting sick of this reunion."

Mo turned to Blair, "I wrote to my children and grandchildren about you, Blair. I knew you would do something miraculous and I wanted it to be in a storybook, like the ones we used to read."

Blair was touched. She pointed at Sybille, "There she is, Mo. This is Sybille, the girl I wrote to in the diaries."

Sybille was touched by their connection.

Jewel drifted upward and made a calling sound.

Mo stepped out of Mancy. He addressed Mancy, "I'm your grandfather, well great, great... and I can't stay."

A swarming sound rushed through the tunnel and Michael flew up to meet the demons Jewel had called in.

Bea was strapped to the surgical table. She watched as the doctors prepared the instruments that would be inserted through her nostrils into her brain.

Perhaps it was finally time to give in. She closed her eyes and heard Frank's voice. It was soothing and familiar. Thoughts of Frank and Salvatore could certainly ease any pain.

"Snap out of it, Bea," Frank shook her.

Bea looked up to see Frank. "What?"

"It's time," Frank assured her. "Paul will help us."

She looked over to see the very enthusiastic Paul standing behind the doctors.

Eston had announced to the world that they chant three words should they become frightened or feel despair in the coming hours: "Bless our world."

He knew they wouldn't understand prayer and he hadn't time to explain.

IT'S TIME

Michael nodded to Blair. The time had come for Sybille to make her move.

Michael slayed the immediate demons Jewel had summoned into the tunnel and he needed Sybille to surface and fulfill her mission.

"It's time," Blair told Sybille.

Jewel flew out to the surface and called her squadron of hellhounds.

Sybille was panicking. She didn't know what they wanted her to do, "Tell me…"

Baker awakened groggily and could see her daughter talking to someone she couldn't see.

Crystal, Mark and Zahndra were passed out and Jewel and Mancy were missing.

Another quake ripped through the building and the lights began to flicker and walls crack. A stampede of bodies were rushing from the cavernous tunnel halls toward them. It was mass panic and soon all were racing past and moving toward the only exit they knew of, the elevators. Others panicked and moved down to the caverns.

Blair and Joan stood with Sybille, "We're beside you all the way."

Sybille heard the screams and saw the demons that chased the Thirdshifters. She turned to her mother, "Is there another way out?"

Baker nodded and they worked to rouse the others. Once Crystal, Zahndra and Mark were up, Baker led Sybille and the others through the elevator repair shafts and got ahead of the tunnel people.

They surfaced in advance of the Thirdshifters. Zahndra radioed Eston for backup. Since it was early winter, the tunnel people would be spared the blinding sunlight, but would be startled by the masses above and the low temperatures.

Panic from the earthquake was rippling through the city and the subways were beginning to flood.

When the first wave of white uniforms emerged, many were bruised and bleeding from the stampede. The Peace Doctors and Entertainment Ministers corralled them into a nearby museum that was dark for an exhibit change.

The surface personnel were startled by the body deformities and blood.

"How will we ever contain the infections?" The doctors were beginning to buckle under the enormity of the situation.

The people kept coming, filling the streets, and with no outer garments they were shivering from the drastic climate change.

Sybille, Blair and Joan moved quickly to Skyline Park. Baker wanted to find Abner and separated from the group. Zahndra and Mark positioned themselves under Crystal's shoulders, carrying her toward Global Good headquarters.

The sound of a jet flying over the city brought more screams of hysteria.

It wasn't a jet, but a pack of demons flying in solidarity. They had been awakened from centuries of hibernation and were wildly vicious. Soon they would begin possession of the weak.

Jewel zoomed ahead of them and perched next to Sybille on the Skyline Bridge. "Wanna fly?"

She grabbed Sybille and sent her tumbling off the structure.

Michael swooped in and caught Sybille, setting her down carefully as he raised his sword to meet Jewel in flight. "Call them off."

"You call off the saints!" Jewel spat.

"What do you want?"

"Same thing you want Michael, to be in control."

"I'm defender of God's people." Michael boomed.

Sybille moved toward the park exit to find the others and get to safety.

"Well you're lousy at it!" Jewel laughed. "You're the one who caused the quake that disrupted the Tunnel. I was just going to stir up some fun down there and kill you. But look at this!" She cackled proudly, "Who says you don't have the devil in you." She stopped on the parkway and skipped a little. "I think you're kind of sweet on me, too why else this lovely gift?"

He grit his teeth and didn't respond.

"I mean, I'm predisposed to the fallen status. But it looks like you want to join us."

"I am not a serpent," Michael spat.

"We're done with all this Good." She danced around him at tornado speed, causing more screams from the people below.

"Your grandmother didn't give up her status to fall from grace. She did so out of love." Michael reminded her.

"Did she? Or is that the story you want to believe?" Jewel mocked.

Michael drew his sword, prepared to swing it at Jewel's long white neck.

Mancy screamed from below, "Don't! She's my sister!"

Michael's sword was swept out of his hand and the force of 1,000 demons swarmed around him, carrying him off.

Blair and Joan materialized in front of Jewel. Joan kissed her sword and tossed it to Blair.

Blair hesitated. "I thought this was Sybille's battle?" She didn't want to fight. She watched Michael struggling with the demon cloud that was moving away from them. She knew Joan wanted her to end Jewel's evil destruction. She now understood what Michael meant about not wanting to fight, but having to.

"Yeah," Jewel chimed in. "It doesn't seem saintly to fight." Jewel reached for the sword Blair held.

"Sybille has a long battle ahead, Blair." Joan urged Blair to toss her the sword.

"Girls, girls let's work together." Jewel reasoned. "Michael's gone. You're not beholden to anyone." Jewel grabbed again.

Blair tossed the sword back to Joan.

Joan without hesitation plunged the sword into Jewel's heart and the holy weapon shriveled up in her chest cavity to soon become a part of Jewel and end the vile beast. Blair moved away from the fallen angel, not wanting to encounter any part of her aura.

Jewel's scream thundered out and she fell with the weight of a torpedo to earth, striking and crushing Mancy as he tried to catch her. Their bodies were entwined in a twisted wreath of limbs and flesh.

Blair hadn't expected Mo's grandson to die this way, or die at all. She was saddened by the sight. But then she watched as Mancy's spirit lifted up to meet Mo.

Mancy was lead by Mo's light.

"Mancy tried to save his sister, not a demon. It's okay Blair," Mo called to her. "He's with me now."

Blair waved to them. She knew Mancy would be at peace.

Sybille was inconsolable at the noise and violence and began chanting Michael's name as she was stopped in her tracks by enormous grief. She didn't know how the winged man would help them now. She feared he'd be destroyed by the demons.

Frank and Paul materialized beside her.

"We can't live like this," Sybille was distraught by the pandemonium.

"We're here with you," Paul assured Sybille.

She moved out of the way of the crowds who were pushing their way to the bridges.

"Frank and I are saints. So are Blair and Joan. If you pray and ask us to help you, we will."

"Help us now." Sybille begged. Her tears welling in desperation.

"We are."

"I only see destruction and frightened people." Sybille was confused. "How can this be better than Good? What am I supposed to do? What is this mission? *Tell me!*"

"There is a higher power."

"Blair told me in her diaries and now our world is destroyed. How does this God make sense?" She was beyond herself.

Bea found Sybille and tried to explain, "Remember when you heard the elevator the day I took you in?"

Sybille nodded.

"Remember that splinter that pricked your finger and brought you off the ledge," Bea reminded her. "You also asked for help, if anyone was listening. Your prayer was heard."

Sybille's eyes got big.

"That wood splinter is a symbol. Like a thorn," Bea continued. "The pain of thorns should never be forgotten. My saintly mission was to house you once Blair's diary was released so that you might find your way. I am more earthbound. Blair, Frank, Joan and Paul are spirit."

Paul chimed in, "Regarding these demons that frighten you today, fear not, for it is written: 'Lord, in your name even the demons submit to us! Nevertheless, do not rejoice at this, that the spirits submit to you, but rejoice that your names are written in heaven.'"

"Heaven." Sybille like the way the word sounded, freeing and calming.

"Heaven," Paul echoed.

Bea continued, "You felt pain in that splinter. God wanted you to choose life and even if you had not, he would have brought you home to heaven."

"If I hadn't opened Blair's diary?" Sybille needed to know.

Frank stepped closer and put his hand under her chin. "God called you Sybille, and he did so through Blair. He would care for you if you hadn't found the diary. It seems this world started to mirror God's word, "God saw everything that he had made, and indeed, it was very good... 'And God saw the light was **GOOD**; And God separated the light from the darkness.'"

"The shifts!" Sybille said.

"There are a lot of things God said are good, and," Frank said, "these people started out good, but a house divided cannot stand. You have to respect all people and they each have talents to share with one another."

At that moment Blair materialized next to Sybille. "Michael got free and slayed most of the demons who captured him, but a small sect are moving toward Region 3."

"Blair I have to know, who repaired the ledge so I wouldn't be detected?" Sybille asked.

Blair looked at Paul and Frank, smiling, "A carpenter we know."

"But how could I enter something into Zahndra's keycard, it's programmed for her?" Sybille wanted concrete answers.

Blair laughed, "I don't have all the answers Sybille, but I can tell you that whenever the impossible happens, it's because someone is divinely looking out for you."

In a blink all the saints were gone and Sybille felt a hand on her waist. In her ear a soft male voice said, "We have work to do. I need you to come with me."

Sybille faced the handsome man whose hair was smudged gray at the temples. She looked at his uniform and it didn't match either shift and she wondered who made it? She loved the tailoring.

She nodded.

His touch gave her a warm feeling and she asked, "Could I let my parents know where I am … and my friends, please?" Her eyes pleaded with his.

"Your parents and brother know you're with me, and Crystal and Zahndra are with them."

"I don't have a brother." Sybille corrected Eston.

"Mark is your brother. He searched the GoodEgg Bank looking for his biological mother and discovered he was working with her. That's why he was bothering you. He wanted to see what kind of a mother Baker really is."

"Eggtraction," she seemed to realize. "But how do we know who our siblings are?"

"They reside on the opposite shift," he said reluctantly, "You may as well know, that's why changes aren't allowed."

"But you said Mark worked with mother?"

"He's in Quad support and not actually on Baker's shift. This is a rare occurrence and it's not like a sibling and sibling union would happen."

"Oh." Sybille seemed distracted in thought.

Eston wondered about the tape he'd seen from 9.14. In its grainy pixelization he wondered what brought such a beautiful woman to such a state of despair.

"They are waiting for us," Eston reassured. "You will be leading us in prayer."

"You know the saints?"

Eston shook his head, "I met a few, but I don't know them. You can teach me."

Blair, Frank, Paul, Michael and Joan rematerialized to Sybille and waved goodbye.

Sybille began to choke up and Eston wasn't certain why.

She didn't want these new friends to leave.

"We are never gone," Blair said to Sybille. She gave Sybille a hug of light. "You can call on us anytime. We are intercessors and we help people. We could be busy. So be patient."

"But, I still don't understand God?" Sybille said to Blair.

Eston just watched Sybille. He didn't understand her motions and discussion, but at the moment there was a lot he didn't understand.

"He's going to help you," Blair pointed at Eston.

"I will miss you, Blair," Sybille said. She turned to Eston and put her head on his shoulder and wept. He gave her a reassuring hug and motioned to Bea to come along with them.

The crowd continued to push them. He placed a hand on each of Sybille's shoulders and looked into her eyes, "You will be giving a Global announcement shortly. I'll be right beside you."

READING GROUP
DISCUSSION QUESTIONS

1. Why was the date 9/14 used? What historic events on 9/14 lead the author to choose this date?
   Hint: 9/14/1936, 9/14/2001 and 9/14/2008 are prominent.

2. What does 9/14 symbolize?

3. Why was the color gray prominent?

4. Why would the author choose St. Paul as the religious figure vs. another religious figure?

5. What letters or writings from ancestors have you read?

6. Have you asked a saint for intercessory prayer? What happened?

7. Why do you think the author chose Michael vs. another angel, like Gabriel to protect Blair?

8. Do you think it would be better to live in Global Good's world than the present world?

9. Why was the eight-year-old girl never seen by anyone but Eston? Who or what do you think she was?

10. Why was the number 86 used for the holding cell?

11. How do you feel about eating alternative meats?

12. Have you discovered your true talent?

13. Where do you think talent comes from?

14. What does Bea mean, when she said the: "The pain of thorns should never be forgotten"?

ACKNOWLEDGEMENTS

I started tracing back the beginning of the plot line for *St. Blair* and realized it all started when I was carrying our daughter Blair. I had finished writing the first novel named for her sister Marquel and was developing the setting for the next. At this writing, both girls are now in their twenties and working in the film industry in California.

At the time, I didn't realize I was developing a young adult paranormal with steam punk influences as the genre didn't exist then. However, I might be pioneering the "saint" genre? With vampires and zombie reaching a saturation point, it might be time for a new species to emerge.

My day job is sales and I'm quite the go-getter in my work, but as a writer, I'm more reserved. It was my daughters who inspired me to reignite my writing career.

Blair is our filmmaker and Marquel our actress. Together they created a booktrailer for my adult novel *Marquel* in 2012 with actor Eric Roberts (which is up on YouTube—search Marquel booktrailer). It's been available in print since 2001 and in recent years I had it converted to the ebook platforms. With the ebook and booktrailer, *Marquel* is relevant again.

I wrote *Marquel* shortly after the death of my mentor, Harry Whittington. Harry was one of the masters of the earliest mass-market paperback originals. The pulps. He taught me to plot and gave me a thumbs-up on the first novel's outline and sample chapter shortly before he died.

I challenged myself to write as Harry had a chapter a day and *Marquel* was written in 53 days. I was also working a job that had major down time and that allowed me to write for hours uninterrupted.

St. Blair was written in coffee shops and on my porch away from the demands of work. I started three years ago on weekends only. It was not outlined initially, but washing around in my head. Not only was this a genre that I didn't understand or know existed, but it was a story I had to write.

St. Blair is for young adults vs. *Marquel* that has adult language and situations.

I am extremely grateful to my sister Ellen Williams who edited both books; Rebecca Rose Hofmann who designed the original *St. Blair* ebook cover and a new friend I met on Twitter; Bunny Cates for being generous with her time and advice; Lisa DeSpain who is also a Twitter acquaintance that formatted the print and ebook; as well as good friends Amy Green, Robyn Fairbanks, Ralph Hamblin, Kim Salter, Pritam Shah, my daughters Marquel and Blair, and a new Facebook friend, Suleika Santana who each have read the book at various stages and provided honest feedback.

I know people will wonder what kind of mother or writer would think up such a crazy concept as to incorporate her daughters' names into novel titles and storylines. I'm not so sure, myself. It added an enormous amount of pressure and that's partially why this has taken so long. When I was younger, I didn't know any better. Now I'm like, what heck was I thinking?

ABOUT THE AUTHOR

 Emily Skinner lives in Tampa Bay, Florida with her middle school math teacher husband, Tom. In addition to writing, she also enjoys selling advertising, antiquing, and working with their daughters, Marquel Skinner and Blair Skinner on their film and acting projects.

Upcoming works include:
The sequel to *Marquel* titled *Marquel's Dilemma*
2 more books in the *St. Blair: Children of the Night* trilogy
St. Blair: Sybille's Reign
The Diary of St. Blair

You may reach Emily by writing to:
Emily W. Skinner
PO Box 8590
Seminole, FL 33775-8590
emily@emilyskinneradvertising.com
Follow Emily at:
http://thefilmmom.blogspot.com/
www.twitter.com/emilyauthor

Made in the USA
Charleston, SC
28 April 2014